Scream of the Silent Sun

Dianna Sinovic

dsinovic610@gmail.com

CONNECT with the publisher:

ParisianPhoenix

ParisBirdBooks

parisianphoenix

Chapter 1

Rain can be a metaphor for deep sorrow and endless tears. For me, the driving rain that soaked my shoes and flooded the road outside my parents' house foretold all the heartbreak that would follow.

I was standing in my parents' house for the first time in more than a decade. By crossing the threshold, it was as though I had stepped back into my eighteen-year-old self, just before I'd walked out the door for the last time.

I had wanted to say no, leave me alone, I have my own life now. But my father insisted, calling me at work, interrupting a client meeting. My mother needed to see a specialist at Penn.

"Just two days," he said. "That's all I ask. You owe it to her."

I owed her nothing after what they'd done, but with my client giving me pointed looks, I ended the call after agreeing to take the time off.

As I stood in the foyer, Gideon the terrier circling at my bare feet, my soggy shoes next to the door, my father handed me the house keys. "We should be back by Friday afternoon, God willing," he said. The self-righteous face I remembered creased into worry lines, anxiety pouring off him. Gray dusted his temples. My mother's face was closed. She nodded slightly at my father's pronouncement, pain radiating from her. It had been more than ten years, but I could still read them without effort. Both of them were terrified of what the tests would show.

When they turned out of the driveway, I drank in the quiet interrupted by Gideon's paws clattering on the foyer's tile. I shook off the feeling that time had slipped backward. No, I was still an adult, no longer a teen under their thumb. With Gideon at my heels, I padded through the rooms of the rancher. Nothing had changed. My old bedroom still had the poster of Nirvana tacked above the bed, and my brother's had his favorite bedspread, the one with Han Solo holding a ray gun. I shivered. Were these shrines to our former selves?

The mid-March rain had not let up. I hooked the leash on Gideon, slipped on my damp shoes, and pulled on my hooded jacket. Halfway around the block, Candi texted me. *Coast clear?*

Yes, I sent.

No way was I going to spend more than a few minutes alone in my parents' home. The memories crowded my head, each a reminder of why I had left. Candi had volunteered to keep me company to stave off the ghosts. It was her day off.

I dried Gideon with a towel on the porch and took another walk through the house. What was I looking for? I lingered in Parker's bedroom, touching the spines of the adventure tales and art books he loved, running my hand over the bedspread, opening the closet to look at the rack that held only empty hangers. A sadness settled over me. Where was he? He'd run away at sixteen. Why he'd run was my secret.

"You've got a leak up here," Candi called from the hallway. I closed the closet door, startled. I hadn't heard her come in. "Maybe a pipe in the ceiling? I can call a plumber."

I joined her in the hallway, and my friend and I both gazed up at the drip forming above our heads. I shook off the idea that the house was crying for Parker, too. I found a bucket and positioned it to catch the water.

"I'll bet it's the roof," I decided. We made our way down the stairs and into the kitchen. The steady rain spattered against the windows. "Let me find a flashlight and I'll check the attic."

Armed with a small penlight I'd found in a kitchen drawer, I opened the attic door, sure I would wade into a pool of water somewhere in that gloom. Instead, the air felt faintly electrified, even though there was no dampness anywhere I could see. I was surrounded by the usual detritus of an attic—old, taped cardboard boxes scrawled with "books" and "extra linens" and the forgotten toys of childhood. The tattered Cabbage Patch doll I'd slept with when I was seven, a naked Barbie without a head—had that been Parker's? I scanned the dim room with the slim beam of the penlight and stepped forward to explore. The nicked secretary halfway across the wooden planking drew me, pulled me to it. The ornately carved top piece, the beveled glass doors, the squat, bowed feet. I didn't remember it, but it was the source of the energy that filled the room. Or, maybe it was just me imagining. I do have an unwanted ability to read people's emotions, but it doesn't work on inanimate objects.

Reaching out, I intended to touch one of the glass doors, but my hand was directed lower, to the bottom of three drawers. Puzzled, I angled the penlight to better see, and pulled on the drawer. It stayed put, but the electrified air took on an urgency. It was important that I open the drawer. I pulled again, tugging with more force. The secretary creaked and whined, and the drawer inched out. Open me, it seemed to shout. I considered returning downstairs to get Candi's help. I gave the drawer one more fierce tug, and it opened several more inches. Not fully open but far enough to peer inside.

Nestled in the recess were stacks of envelopes, canceled postage, the ink of the handwriting faded in the penlight's glow. I pulled out a handful and leafed through them, and blinked several times to be sure. My name was on the envelopes. All of them. I had never seen them before, yet all had been opened. What were they doing here?

I cradled the bundle in one arm, leaving the secretary drawer ajar, and hurried to the kitchen to take a better look. Candi stood in front of the open fridge, glumly eyeing the contents. I'd invited her for lunch, but apparently the food options were limited.

"Look at this." I spilled the letters onto the table and pulled up a chair.

"Ruined by the leak?" she said, still in front of the fridge.

"Worse than that, I think." I looked at the return address on the envelopes and my heart stopped. Parker Thomas. My brother. He hadn't broken his promise after all.

Candi gave up on the fridge and started opening cupboards. "Quinn, what do your parents do for food?" Exasperation tinged her words.

"They—they never told me that he wrote." I felt at sea, calculating the time span represented by the canceled stamps. The first letter was shortly after he ran away, and the last a good five years ago.

I laid my fingers across the ink, across my name written by Parker, trying to pick up some tiny grain of life. Something had pulled me to that drawer. Had he called to me somehow?

Candi picked up one of the envelopes and studied it. "Old love letters? From before Jude?"

"No. From my brother."

"The long-lost bro?" Candi pulled a folded paper from the envelope she held. She knew about Parker, that he'd vanished, that I had no idea where he was. My brother was exotic lore, the kind of dysfunction cred that can be traded among friends who are thankful that it doesn't directly affect them.

"Parker sent these letters to me, but my mom intercepted them."

Candi turned the envelope over in her hand. "How do you know it was your mother? Maybe your dad? Are you sure you didn't just stash these upstairs and forget about them?"

"It wasn't my dad," I said flatly. He would have left them in the mailbox rather than bring them into the house. And the later letters had been sent after I'd left home, yet my mother had not forwarded them to me.

The envelopes had been slit open with care, not a ragged edge among them, and the letters within had been folded and refolded over and again. My mother could easily have burned them when they arrived, unwelcome, but she had hidden them away instead, apparently making a regular pilgrimage to the attic to reread them. I opened the first one that my brother had sent.

I could hear his voice, the cadence of his words as he gave details about the friend's place he was staying at, sleeping on the floor, the part-time job he'd stumbled upon, his plans to get a GED and try the local community college in the fall. I wondered how much he had changed. Would I recognize him if he walked through the door? Why had my mother kept these from me?

"So you didn't know these letters existed?" Candi placed a plate of cheese, crackers, and apple slices on the table. While I was eating up the letters, she had rummaged through enough drawers to pull together a passable lunch for us.

"Nope." I shook my head and reached for a cracker, considering how much to reveal. "My parents told me he ran away because he hated school." The real story was that they forced him into a corner and running was his only way out. But he had vowed that he would write or call. "Don't worry," he'd said to me shortly before he ran. "You're my little sis, QT," using his pet name for me. "I won't forget you."

In that time before emails made staying in touch so easy, he hadn't written, and he hadn't called. I waited eagerly at first, then worriedly, and then as the months and years passed, resignedly. I kept his secret, moved out, graduated from college. And stopped waiting. I had no idea where Parker was. Yet if he'd written these letters to me, he was out there somewhere. I teased the edge of an envelope and sighed. "The truth is much different."

"Then let's dig into these and see what they say." Candi, who jokes that her middle name is Organized, divided the stack in half, taking a portion for herself and sat down across from me. "Your parents won't be back today."

I was just unfolding the third letter when Jude called. "We've got to talk."
I started to answer, "Sure—about what?" But he spoke over me.
"Meet me at the coffeeshop." Then he ended the connection.
Jude could be moody. It was one of the traits that attracted me to him initially. That shifting pattern of emotions was fascinating, so different from my more even temperament. I chalked up his terseness to that and felt annoyed. I wanted to read every last letter right then, immersing myself in Parker's life, not stand down Jude, as much as I loved him.

I bundled the letters into two stacks and wrapped each with a rubber band. I wasn't stealing them. They were mine. Together Candi and I locked up the house.

"Let me know what happens," she said with an air kiss.

I met Jude at the coffeeshop in New Hope that we liked. Three tables in the rear and three stools in the window. He was in a window seat. That should have been my first clue to what was coming. I slid onto the stool next to his.

His hands gripped the wooden counter that spanned the window. He wore the gray wool sweater that I'd given him last Christmas, the one that matched his eyes. Staring out the window, he watched the passersby on the sidewalk. His shoulders were stiff, his jaw set. *I'm not budging*, his attitude said, but vibrating from him was an undercurrent of anxiety. That should have been my second clue.

"I'm here," I said. "What's on your mind?" The moment those words left my lips I wanted to take them back.

"None of your fucking business, Quinn," he said. But he spoke softly, intently — still not looking at me. "That's the issue."

"There's an issue?" My tone was light, but my stomach knotted.

"Jude!" The barista called out the order, and Jude went to the register to pick it up. He placed a mocha espresso in front of me and sat down with a cappuccino.

Was this a peace offering of some sort? Mocha espresso was my very favorite.

"Thanks," I said. I wrapped my hands around the paper cup. "So."

Keeping his face to the window, Jude sipped from his cup, then sighed. "This is so hard."

"Jude — what is it? What's going on?" I reached out and touched his arm.

He turned and looked at me squarely, then dropped his gaze.

"We have a good thing going," he said, sighing again. "I like you. But there's something weird about you. That you always seem to know what I'm thinking. Sometimes I don't even know what I'm thinking until you voice it. It's unnerving."

Just as my three previous flames had informed me. Maybe it was my fate to always lose at love. But this was Jude. Not Jude, too.

"Yes," I said softly. "It's always that way."

"What way?" The coffeeshop was crowded, and it was hard to hear the nuance in his voice over the noise, but I could feel his anxiety washing over me.

"This isn't the best place to have this discussion," I said. "Can we get out of here?"

He shook his head, glancing to the rear of the shop, where we usually sat. "No, I've got to say this right here, right now, even though it hurts."

Then I knew. "Please, Jude." I didn't want to plead, but there I was. "Let's talk about this." My touch on his arm became a grasp, as though I could hold him in place.

"I need a break. Time away from your eerie sense." He stood. "And I'm sure you need a break from me. Then we'll see where it goes."

Meaning he had already decided, and the way it would go would be nowhere.

"Sorry," he said. He gently pulled my fingers from his arm, brushed my cheek with his lips, and was gone before I could process the movement.

I stared at the empty stool and the half-empty cup of cappuccino, now cooling with no one to finish it.

Chapter 2

I've been "odd" my whole life, or cursed, depending on your viewpoint. Jude's rejection was only the latest blow, but it still ripped a hole in me. We had made it two years, the longest span yet for a relationship—so things were improving, if I wanted to look at it that way. I didn't. I cried all the way to my condo.

Remember Parker, I reminded myself. The cache of letters sat on the passenger seat, expectant. I could push Jude aside for a few hours while I read the rest of my brother's correspondence.

After dumping the stack on the table, I put on a pot of coffee and turned up the volume on Slayer. I lay on the floor in my living room, letting the music wash over me, my mind filled with images of Jude. The first time we'd met, on the towpath, me with a flat on my bike and he with his piercing eyes and heartthrob face offering to give me a lift home. The tender way he held me, running his finger lightly over my cheekbones before kissing me. The hours we'd spent watching old movies together, including *Rear Window,* our favorite. The DVD sat on top of my TV, ready for another viewing. I felt like Jeff, immobilized and helpless, while Lars Thorwald tried to get away with murder. Jude was no criminal, but he had stolen my heart.

With a mug of coffee beside me, I pushed away Jude and sorted through the letters again. More than two dozen with nearly as many postmarks. California, Arizona, Colorado, Minnesota, Pittsburgh, Boston. The latest, from five years ago, were from New York. He'd written most often when he had moved.

I'm in Boulder now. Staying with a friend of a friend. You can reach me here for probably the next six months. I seem to be a good fit for sandwich shops — it's the fifth one I've worked in as many cities. The art is going well. I may get a contract for a new mural.

In most of the letters, Parker had included sketches of people and places, ideas for murals, oddball signs he'd noted. I was proud of his art but also jealous. I'd missed out on so much of his life.

Candi showed up at the condo with take-out dinner from the Italian deli she frequented.

"Real food," she said, reminding me of the meager cheese-and-cracker lunch at my parents' house. "Lasagna was the special today." She placed the Styrofoam container on the table, plus a container of salad. "How are you holding up?"

I brought in plates and flatware, and two bottles of beer. "I'll live." I hoped so, but right then, my body ached as though I'd been pummeled.

She gave me a hug. "I know it hurts. But you're tough. You'll get through this. I liked Jude, but you're my friend, he's not. I've already ripped his picture from my mental photo album."

For me, it wouldn't be as easy. "I should've seen it coming," I said, picking at my lasagna. "They all end that way for me, but I'd really, truly hoped he was the one."

"The letters," Candi said, tapping the stack. "Try to forget Jude for now. Did you finish them?"

"Almost." I knew she was eager to read the letters herself. As a research librarian, she took as a challenge any situation that involved tracking down missing information.

Finished with dinner, we pushed the plates aside and I laid the letters out on the table.

Too soon, I had only one letter left. I hesitated, reluctant to reach the end. With each missive, I had waited to feel something. I sighed, turning the last letter over in my hands.

"What's wrong?" Candi looked up from one of the letters I'd already read.

"I keep hoping for something more with these." I reached into the envelope and pulled out the folded letter. "But it's just paper. Nothing special that I can pick up."

"Your super sense?" Candi knows about me, and mostly puts up with it. That's why she's been a friend since college.

"Yeah," I said. "It's stupid of me to wish that."

"At least you found the letters, girl. Be thankful for that." She scrunched into a frown. "Most of us don't read minds."

"I don't…," I started, but then simply nodded. We'd been through this argument endless times.

I unfolded the final letter, the one postmarked from Brooklyn. Parker wrote of yet another impending move. By this time, he was in his mid-twenties, hanging out with a handful of other artists. He loved the energy of the borough, the wildness of eastern Long Island, drawn to both, he said, by the ever-shifting light. But it was hard to make a living there. He was casting off again, wherever the sun led him.

Still no letters from you. You're out of college now by my reckoning. Whatever lies Mom and Dad told you about me I guess you believed. Ask Braden for the real story.

The letter ended, as all the others had, with Parker's signature, the entwining P and T.

I kept my promise, I argued. *I know the real story.*

I passed the letter on to Candi. "Braden was Parker's best friend growing up."

She read it quickly and refolded it, pushing it back across the table. "And the lies?"

"It's complicated." I was reluctant to share that part of Parker's past without his permission.

Candi collected the plates to take them to the kitchen. "That's life, isn't it? Tell me when you're ready."

And I would, eventually.

I cleaned up the kitchen, and Candi left to get in a spin workout.

At the table, I looked at each envelope yet again, hoping I had missed a letter, one dated more recently. Had he really given up writing to me? Or had my mother stuck later letters elsewhere?

I drove to my parents' house that evening with two goals. I fed Gideon and took him for another walk, the rain still pelting us and Stone Temple Pilot's "Vasoline" playing on my iPod. With the dog dried off and now inside the warmth of the house, I found a better flashlight in my parents' garage. Returning to the attic, I scoured the secretary for more letters and looked in a nicked, three-drawer chest and pried open a battered trunk. Nothing. No letters, not a flicker of extrasensory energy.

Parker, where are you?

Thursday morning, I was at work, able to push both Jude and Parker out of my thoughts for a few hours. My first client canceled, giving me time to complete some overdue paperwork before the weekly staff meeting.

At ten o'clock, I joined the rest of the staff in the conference room, a small, tired space with mismatched chairs and a hand-me-down table from the former ad agency next door. Someone before my time had tried to add a bit of cheer by hanging travel posters—to Hawaii, France, India, Japan. They just served to remind me that our limited salaries would never allow us to travel to any of those picturesque places.

"People," Amanda Reed said, opening the staff meeting with her usual greeting. "You are doing great work, as always." She looked around the table at me and the seven other counselors, as we waited for the punchline. The anxiety from around the table rose in intensity and pitch. "But I have some unfortunate news. The General Assembly—"

Heywood interrupted. "The bastards have done it again?"

Amanda Reed frowned. "Jeremiah," she said. "Please let me—"

Another counselor spoke up. "Christ, pretty soon, we'll be able to make more money at K-Mart."

"I haven't—" Amanda Reed tried again.

"We're also talking about our clients' *lives*," Heywood said.

"They don't care," I said. It was a story we'd all heard too many times—addicts and alkies deserved what they got.

Slipping off her black pump, Amanda Reed hammered the heel on the table, bringing the meeting back to order.

"You are correct in your assumption," she said. "The General Assembly has cut funding. It's the third year in a row. Unfortunately, it means you all will be making less if you stay here. I'll do my best to see that our clients won't be affected."

"Are we supposed to work for free?" Heywood grumbled as he and I walked to our offices. "I've got a mortgage. We all have bills to pay."

Money had been a struggle since I started counseling, but I could never give it up. I'd found a niche where I could tap into my deeper sense and use it for good. Somehow I would scrimp even more and keep hoping I'd never have to decide between survival and my career.

Thursday slipped into Friday. Jude haunted my dreams—he was always just beyond reach—but my insomnia and restless sleep were nothing new. His absence just made them more draining.

Over my lunchbreak on Friday, I drove to my parents' house to walk the dog and found their car parked in the driveway. I could have just dropped the key in the mailbox and left, but I had questions that needed to be answered. Letting myself in with the key, I stepped into a deep silence and pulsing sadness.

My mother sat at the kitchen table, and my father leaned against a counter. They both had mugs of coffee, but they simply held their cups, staring at nothing. My father's six-foot height and large hands made his mug seem small.

"What did you find out from Penn?" I said. Gideon barked once to acknowledge me and settled on the floor next to my mother, his favorite of the room's occupants.

My father turned to me, surprised to find me there. The blank look on his face reassembled into the sternness I had grown up with. "Inconclusive," he said. "We go back next week for another round of tests."

A tear welled in my mother's eyes. She shook her head very, very slightly. As in so many past instances, my father was choosing to ignore the truth and my mother acquiesced with silence. It had been ten years, but they were following the same script.

I mentally thumbed through the symptoms they'd shared with me. Recurring headaches, nausea, twitching in her right arm, blurry vision—and her mood, as though something was off-balance in an incremental way. I'm an addiction counselor not a doctor, but those were textbook symptoms of a brain tumor.

"More tests?" If my father refused to accept the diagnosis, this would be his way of putting off the reality, insisting on a second opinion despite seeing one of the top neurologists in the region. "There's a leak in the roof," I added lamely. "I put a bucket in the hallway upstairs."

But my father didn't seem to hear me. Putting his mug in the sink, he went into his study and shut the door.

"Mom?" I sat down across from her. She had closed her eyes. Whatever they'd been told had shaken them to their roots.

"Four months," she said, her words faint even in the quiet of the kitchen.

I reached for her hand, the hand that had hoarded my brother's letters for all those years, and held it.

Chapter 3

"I found something that needs an explanation." I gripped my mother's hand, wavering between anger and profound sadness. I was torn between wanting to wait until another day and demanding an answer right then.

"Go ahead," my mother said. "But not about today, not yet…" The deep sadness that flowed off her mixed with my own sorrow. It was hard to tell where hers ended and mine began.

I shook my head. "No, not about today. It's something else." I tried to be gentle, but I had to know. I described my search in the attic and what I'd found. "All this time, I thought Parker had abandoned me. But he cared. He kept his promise—and you let me think he hadn't."

My mother pulled her hand from mine but said nothing for a few moments. "I meant to burn them."

"So I would *never* have known? I could have had a real brother all those years instead of just a memory. You had no right to keep my letters. They were *mine*. He's my *brother*."

Again my mother said nothing for several moments. "It's not what you think," she said finally.

"The last of his letters in that drawer were from five years ago," I said. "Has he written since then? Tell me the truth."

My mother's lips trembled. "I'm so, so sorry." She pointed to the living room. "The Bible on the bookshelf. Bring it."

I laid it on the kitchen table, and she opened it to the Book of Amos. Nestled within was another letter. Unopened. She handed it to me.

The moment my fingertips touched the paper, an emotional current sizzled them, and I jerked my hand away. *Was this energy from my mother? Parker?*

"What's wrong?" my mother said. "This is the last one. I just couldn't open it."

I cautiously tried to pick up the letter again. This time the jolt was gentler. Turning the envelope over and over, I puzzled at my reaction. This was a letter, not a person. Why did I feel energy from it?

When I slipped a finger under the flap to open it, my mother put her hand out to stop me.

"Not here," she said. "Please." She must have seen the disappointment in my eyes, because she quickly added, "Take it. You're right—they're all yours."

Her shoulders slumped, and she turned her face away from me. "I need to go lie down."

I helped her up the stairs to their bedroom, found sweats for her to change into, and tucked her into bed. Mechanically I brushed her forehead with a kiss. She was burning hot, so I fetched a cool washcloth.

Once she'd settled into a doze, I hurried to the kitchen and used a paring knife to slit open the letter. Before I could remove the contents, my father strode into the room. I stood, envelope and knife in hand.

"What's that?" he said, a challenge in his tone.

I felt time slip backward again, tugging me toward my younger self. "Nothing," I said, squelching a sarcastic response.

He stared at me for a moment, as we reprise roles from long ago. "He who is devious in his ways spurns Him. Proverbs 14:2."

Refusing the bait, I stuck the envelope in my jacket pocket. "Mom's in bed. She said she was tired." I picked up my backpack and walked to the front door. "Your keys," I called, and hung them on the hook beside the entrance.

In the car, I pulled out the envelope. The postmark was Brooklyn again, and the date about a year after the last letter from the attic. Eagerly, I unfolded the letter.

QT — I'm in trouble. If you get this letter, I need your help. I can't explain in a few lines. You'll have to trust me. I trust you.

Parker had underlined *trouble* and *help* in red ink.

I shivered. My brother had begged me for help… four years ago. "Damn it!" I shouted. I pictured him dead or in prison, all because I'd never seen his plea.

My first instinct was to set out for Brooklyn, but with the trail four years cold, the trip could wait. Instead, I returned to the office to finish out my day, my mind unable to focus.

At the stroke of five, I was off to Candi's apartment in New Hope. I dumped the stack of Parker's letters onto her carved wooden coffee table, next to the statue of a griffin. She let me rant about the latest missive while she hung her newest find on the wall near her kitchen table, a replica of a longsword. My best friend might live in the opening years of the twenty-first century, but her heart stood in Medieval England. The lamp over her kitchen table is fashioned after a knight's helmet, and she will slip on a wench's gown to do her laundry. If Arthur walked through her front door, he would feel right at home, between Guinevere the cat and Lancelot the cactus.

Candi's boyfriend, Chad, arrived with pizza. I got out plates and napkins while Candi opened the beer, and the three of us sat at her small oak dining table, passing around the pizza box.

"So what do I do?" I said, biting into a slice of plain cheese. "I wonder why he didn't call if he needed my help that badly."

"Maybe he did but it was your parents' house and he hung up when you didn't answer." Candi tapped a finger on her beer bottle. "He wouldn't have known your cell number."

Chad slid another slice onto his plate. "He was probably broke, and he was hitting you up, making you feel guilty."

"I don't think so," I said. But I wasn't sure. The connection I'd felt to Parker had faded with time and his absence.

Over another beer, I told Chad about the other letters, with Candi adding her own opinions.

"Let me read them," Chad said. "I might be able to offer a different perspective. I know they're personal, but they're not exactly a secret. Candi's read them."

"But—" I wanted to say, *She's my BFF and you're just her latest hope.* I kept my mouth shut. "Sure."

I handed each letter to Chad, carefully refolding each one as he finished it and tucking it safely away in my backpack.

I placed the last letter on the table. "This is the one my mom never opened."

"And the one that's put you in a tailspin," Candi said.

When Chad pulled the letter from its envelope, a slip of stiff paper fell, landing face down in his plate. I snatched it up quickly. How had I missed it when I read the letter earlier?

I turned it over and sucked my breath in. It was an exquisite drawing of the sun, its corona depicted as radiant flames dancing around a fiery yellow center.

"Your brother drew that?" Chad asked, leaning in to get a closer look.

"Yes," I murmured, touching the edges of the paper reverently. It wasn't signed, but my gut knew that this was his careful hand at work.

Candi put her arm around my shoulders and squeezed. "His birthday, right?"

Parker was born on the summer solstice, the longest day of the year, and he adopted the sun as his symbol, his emblem, his fixation. After he ran off, I found his earmarked copy of Whitman's collected poems, the line highlighted, with red ink stars drawn on either side of the page:

Give me the splendid silent sun with all his beams full-dazzling

Where was my splendid silent brother now? He could be next door—or across the world from where I sat—or even, as I shuddered to think, dead and buried.

"That would make an awesome tattoo," Chad said.

"You *would* say that." I laughed, breaking the spell the design seemed to have on us.

Chad has an intricate spider web and menacing black widow on his left shoulder, and a half-man/half-wolf on his right arm, transforming under a full moon. Jude had no tattoos. I have only a screech owl on my right shoulder and the letters BB on my ankle, the second done under circumstances I would rather not recall.

I cupped the slip and laid it, sunny side down, on my forearm. "I could put it here," I joked, "or maybe on my back. The sun would never set on me."

My arm warmed where the slip of paper lay. When I pulled the paper off to return it to the envelope, the symbol had transferred itself, like one of those temporary kids' tattoos, onto my arm. The paper itself was now blank.

"Cool," Candi said. "I wonder how Parker did that." She stood up and began gathering the dinner debris. "Maybe you can get it to last for a day or two."

I got up to help her. "Can I borrow your camera to take a photo of it?" I rubbed the edges of the tattoo. If I were careful, it might last a week. My arm was still warm, and the sun itself seemed to move slightly, as though the ball of fire was seething. I blinked, and the image was still. I stared for several more seconds, but any movement must have been a trick of the light in the room.

Candi returned with her camera. "Hold out your arm, and I'll get a close-up." She took several shots, but frowned when she looked at the results. "Weird."

"Let me see," I said.

"Give me a sec." She made some adjustments and took a few more shots. Peering again at the results, she shook her head. "Unbelievable."

I took the camera from her, and with Chad looking over my shoulder, we both gazed at the small digital screen. It showed several photos of my arm—definitely my arm because of my watchband—but the sun wasn't visible. It just wasn't there.

"What happened to it?" I said. "I don't understand." I felt slightly dizzy. Was this an odd hallucination, like the faint, flickering images that had suddenly appeared in my peripheral vision? "You still see it on my arm, don't you?" When she and Chad nodded, I added, "Maybe it's just the temporary ink Parker used. The camera won't read it."

"Quinn," Chad said. His eyes held a question mark. "I've seen plenty of tattoos, and that one looks pretty permanent to me."

Chapter 4

I was driving to Philadelphia within the hour. As I drove, I kept glancing at the tattoo, or whatever it was. The image seemed to glow on my skin, but the warmth I'd felt earlier had dissipated. Chad directed me to a shop off South Street called Skin Deep. Pinscher would know what the sun tat was, what had happened, he assured me. The words in Parker's letter repeated themselves. *I'm in trouble.* Was this tattoo a further plea for help?

South Street was crowded that night with St. Paddy's Day partygoers. I stopped several people near Third Street and South, asking for directions to the shop. After three people pointed me in three different directions, I gave up and walked south on Third. A hand-lettered sign for the shop was taped to a streetlight pole and pointed down a narrow alley. In the darkness, I followed the arrow to a neon open sign that slowly blinked on and off. I pondered whether this was as good an idea as it had seemed in Candi's apartment, with Chad's confident urging.

Just like in an old black and white movie, a bell above the interior door tinkled as I pushed it open. Inside, the air smelled of incense and pipe tobacco. The overhead fluorescent lights hummed faintly against the absolute quiet. No voices, no music, no sounds at all, except the lights. A broad counter, waist high, cut the room in half. On my side of it, a few plastic chairs lined the wall on either side of the doorway. Across the counter, on the other side of the room, another doorway was cloaked with beads that hung in strands of blue and purple. The place was so still that the beads did not sway. At all. I glanced at the chairs, trying to decide whether to sit and wait for Pinscher or whoever was there to come out, or just leave. The stillness was eerie, and that was not comforting. When I took another look at the counter, a man was standing there. I could swear the beads were still not moving.

"Are you Pinscher?"

The man nodded. He was short and stocky with a lined face, perhaps weathered from too much time in the sun. His eyes were green and seemed to pull me into them. I shook my head briefly to break the connection.

"Are you on the books?" His voice was deep and soft, but commanding.

"Books?"

"What time are you down for?" He opened a thick spiral ledger to a book-marked page. His right hand was inked with an exquisitely detailed crab, its eye stalks on his first and fourth knuckle, the claws on his first and fourth fingers. The crab's eyes moved—or seemed to move, watching me. It was so real, I reached to touch his hand, but pulled back at the last moment, and my face flushed.

"Sorry. Your crab is so … I'm not here for … " Tongue-tied, I stuttered and then simply showed him my arm, where the sun glistened and seemed almost alive.

"Ah," he said, with what I took to be approval. He opened up the counter door, expectant. What could I do but follow him through the beads?

He sat me in a leather chair and put on a pair of magnifying glasses. "May I?" He gestured at my arm, which I turned toward him with a nod. With a gentleness that surprised me, he held my forearm and ran a finger lightly over the tattoo. The crab on his hand swiveled its eyes to look, as well. He hummed a tune softly under his breath. *Shiny Happy People*? The REM song my brother, at thirteen, had played every chance he got. And just like that I was flooded with an image of Parker, an almost-three-dimensional vision of him, not as a teen but as a grown man.

Pinscher raised his eyes to mine. "You sense him, too." It was a statement, not a question.

"You know Parker?" I was incredulous, then incredibly hopeful. "You've seen him?"

He shook his head. "Alas, no. This tattoo is … " He was silent, as if trying to decide how much to tell me.

"Please," I pleaded. "What is happening? Is it real?" I pulled my arm from his grasp and placed my palm over the image. It seemed to flicker under my touch, and I jerked my hand away.

"Oh, yes, it's real," he said. "I've seen only one or two others like it." He took off his magnifiers and rubbed his eyes. "What makes it special is not the tattoo itself, but the skin, the person, it's inked on. You are like a conduit."

"Me? But how could it be inked?" I rubbed at the tattoo. "The sun was just a drawing on a slip of paper two hours ago. Now it's here." I gestured at my arm.

Pinscher's gaze held mild amusement. "As I said, I've seen only one or two others like it." He laid the magnifiers on a table and stood.

"You said I was like a conduit." I stood, too. "Of what?"

He led me through the beads, to the front counter. "You'll know," he said, "when the time comes. For now, keep an eye on it."

But I had more questions. "I still don't understand. My brother's in trouble. Or was. Is this thing some kind of magic?"

His gaze held mine for long moment. "Some say all art is magic, because of what it can conjure."

Then he wished me luck.

I drove north, out of the city, fascinated and repulsed by the sun on my arm. How was this connected to my brother's plea for help? Was it his way of ensuring that I would listen this time? But five years had passed.

On anyone else, I would have admired the tattoo. But I didn't want it, didn't ask for it. And now I was a conduit. Of something. In the brief, shimmering image of Parker from Pinscher's shop, had he been begging me? I couldn't remember. The details were already fading.

At my condo, I unrolled my yoga mat and did a round of stretching and relaxation to Soundgarden.

Afterward, I made myself an omelet and salad, and sat at my computer to eat. An idea had been teasing itself since Parker's shimmering image smiled at me in Pinscher's shop. The last letter I had was from five years ago, but he might turn up in an online search. Candi would be an expert at this, but hell, I could give it a try.

I searched on "Parker Thomas" and found a number of results, none of them my brother. Then I tried "Thomas" and "murals," and came up empty again. And searching on "murals" gave me too many results, most of them offering murals as home decor. Maybe community murals weren't big news, and maybe my brother kept a low profile. I would ask Candi to run a search for me.

I checked emails. Several for a dating site I'd signed up for—but after a quick look at the potential dates, I deleted them all. One from a colleague who'd moved to Ohio, another from a high school friend now in Oregon. I could answer those later. Then my heart skipped a beat. The subject line was equinox in 3. The sender was pthomas.

I moved the cursor to the email to open it, but hesitated. I looked away and then checked again. Still there. I hadn't imagined it. But it might not be Parker. Thomas wasn't exactly a rare surname, and P could be Patti or Phoebe or…My mind filled in a score of P names. The date of spring was something my brother would note. I clicked on Open.

Hey qt. i need a little help. see you soon maybe.

Chapter 5

I stared at the words Parker had written me. Was it coincidence that his email should arrive so soon after I had discovered his letters? I was a conduit, Pinscher said. Would that explain it? And what kind of help did he need, when I had no idea where he was?

My tattoo burned on my arm, and I shivered in response. Strange happenings seemed to be multiplying. My life—my professional one—is based on a world that's quantifiable and predictable. I'm trained to assess and assist my clients based on solid psychological research and practice. The string of current events fell far outside my usual realm, and it unnerved me.

Still, I had an email on the screen in front of me that was real enough. I could have spent the rest of the night writing a reply—there were years of details to catch him up on—but I decided to keep it simple and direct.

I miss you. There's much to tell. How can I help?

The image of my brother that appeared at the tattoo shop had to be true, didn't it? It proved he was still alive—somewhere. In the hazy image, he was still on the thin side, and his curly brown hair was longer and thicker than I remembered. He had filled in, with a broader chest and muscular arms, but his clothing had been ripped and tattered. Why? I yearned to hear his voice, to hug him, to sit on the couch and, over bottles of dark ale, fill him in on the missing years.

I touched my fingertips to my lips and then to the screen for good luck, then pressed Send. Within an instant the message bounced.

The upwelling of hope I'd felt over the last few minutes drained away, leaving me with an emptiness that ached behind my breastbone. I went to bed, willing sleep to come but knowing it was futile.

I see five patients a day, on average, and Toby is on my Monday list, every week at two o'clock, just after my lunch break. He's made strides in the last two months he's been coming to his appointments, but there's still a long way to go. That's the tricky part of addiction. You don't always think you have a problem, and even when you have managed to stay clean, the imp is always whispering in your ear. *Just once won't hurt — you've been good, you deserve it.*

It was just like Toby to zero in on the thing that had kept me awake most of the night.

"You're upset," he said, folding his arms and tucking them in his armpits. "Bad news?"

I kept my face blank but friendly. Therapy sessions are to help my patients face their demons, but many want to avoid the subject by turning the focus on me.

"Nothing that I can't handle," I said, but immediately redirected. "Let's talk about you. How's the job hunt going? How are you feeling about it?"

With the shoulders and chest of the linebacker he once was, Toby can be intimidating to people he's just met. And when he's high, he can be danger-ous. Or so his record indicates. He's never been high in my presence—that would be grounds for dismissal from the program.

Finding a job when you have a record of using and you are the size of a grizzly seemed pretty much impossible for Toby. He shrugged. "Nothing so far." He paused and then seemed to remember my second question. "It sucks. I never knew it would be this hard."

I could have offered a list of places he could try, but the last list I'd handed him he had glanced at and stuffed it in his jeans pocket, most likely never to be removed until it had turned to mush after a trip through a washing machine.

Instead I picked up on a melancholy mood. "Is it Eddi?" When he nodded, I gently asked, "Is she sick again?"

Again a nod.

"She's with your mom still, right?" Toby's wife, already an addict, had run off when Eddi was three years old, leaving Toby to care for his daughter on his own, while struggling to keep afloat financially. A wise woman, Toby's mother intervened and took Eddi into her own home until Toby could get back on his feet. Then recreational drug use slipped into full-bore addiction. Eddi was now four. "I know you want her with you, but the judge says not yet."

I could feel the melancholy leach into a simmering anger. "I've been clean for two months," he growled. "That should count."

"And it does." How my patients wanted to be done with their rehab, to get on with their life. Which was the whole point of the rehab—to be able to get on with their life without dependency. Some mastered it, and others ended up in the obituary column.

Toby's session drew to a close after more brainstorming about potential jobs. We shook hands, as we did after every appointment. My patients call me by first name—I want them to feel at ease—but I insist on the hand shake. It's the only time we touch.

"Whatever it is," Toby said, looking me in the eye for the first time since he'd walked into my office that day, "don't quit. I need to know that you'll be here." Then he stepped into the hallway and was gone.

I didn't plan to quit, but the looming funding cut might force me to make a difficult choice. And then where would Toby and the rest of those on my client list be?

My answering machine was blinking when I got home from work. The rest of the day had been rocky—especially with a new patient who seemed a blend of flake and flammable. I was bone-tired by the time she left, and then had to sit through a two-hour office meeting *and* do paperwork. I changed into my tights and jacket to go for a training ride, but the damn light kept blinking. If I ignored it, the possible message would keep buzzing around in my mind for every block of my route. Instead of relief from the day's stress, I would pile on more. I hit the button to play it.

It was my father. No details, just asking that I call. My stomach churned—this was what I had walked away from all those years ago. Manipulation. Guilt trips. Sanctimoniousness.

Standing in my foyer, in my socks, I phoned him.

"Your mother starts treatment on Wednesday, at Penn," he said. "She'll most likely need to stay there for a few days, for this initial dose."

I absorbed the news and then realized what he needed. "And you want me to watch Gideon again?"

My father sighed. "If it's not too much to ask."

"Of course not. Whatever I can do to help." I tucked a wayward strand of hair behind my ear. "You sound tired."

"I have a feeling this is…" He stopped speaking for a long moment.

The beginning of the end, I finished the sentence to myself, knowing he would not.

"And one thing more," he said finally. "Your mother wants to see you."

"Okay," I said. "I'll come over Wednesday before work, before you head to Philly."

"Tonight, please." Then the line clicked off.

My mother is stoic to a fault, so her request was something I had to acknowledge. I put on my cycling shoes, slipped on my jacket, cranked up Motörhead's "Born to Raise Hell," and biked to the canal and back—my usual six-mile loop—to quiet my mind and prep myself for what I faced. The next few months would be unbearably sad, and although I am a mental health professional, I am no more immune to personal afflictions of the soul than a medical doctor is to the common cold.

My mother rested on the couch in their living room, covered with a light-weight blue blanket I had once used on my bed when I still lived there. It was pilled now, and the seam along one edge had unraveled. She waved me to a nearby stuffed chair. Instead, I dropped to the floor beside her, sitting cross-legged, expectant. The sorrow vibrated off her like mist pouring over a cliff edge, immersing me in it, but she attempted a small smile.

"I'm glad you came," she said softly. Then she sent my father from the room. "This is something I need to talk with Quinn about."

He turned without a word, and the door to his study closed with a distinct thud.

"Dad said you start treatment—"

She interrupted, pushing herself up higher on the couch pillow. "That's not why I asked you to come over," she said firmly. "Yes, I have cancer, and yes, I'll get chemo or radiation or whatever, and I'll be dead before the summer's out, maybe before that even. But—" She held up her hand against my protest. "So..." She seemed to be deciding what words to use. "Those letters you found. Can you find Parker? Before it's too late? He needs to know what happened."

"Know what?" *But I knew, had known since it happened.*

My mother closed her eyes, then said softly, "I argued and argued with Alan, but he would have it no other way."

"Was this before or after Parker ran away?"

She shook her head slightly. "He didn't run away, at least not the way you were told." Her eyes opened then and she looked at me, gauging my reaction.

I simply nodded, wanting to hear her spin. I knew Parker's side of the story. He'd shared it and sworn me to silence.

"It's complicated," she said, as though hearing my thoughts. "It was when the Hewitts lived a few doors down. Parker and their son, Braden, were as thick as thieves. You weren't as close with Tessy."

Because she was bossy and at age ten preferred to dabble with makeup instead of skateboarding in the park. Tessy, I'd heard, was now a buyer for a fashion boutique, a job that suited her well—even if she still wore too much makeup. And Braden—in his letter, Parker had said to look him up, and that was more than a handful of years ago. I had no idea what he was doing now.

"So what happened?" I prompted.

"Your father thought that Parker and Braden..." She lapsed into silence.

"So what?" I said, hissing my words.

"Your father threw him out," my mother said at last. "Banished him, forbade him from ever coming back."

"And you let him." It was cruel to say it, I admit, but they were in this despicable pact together.

"I thought it was for the best," she said. "You must hate me for that, but it was my marriage or my son, and I thought, 'Well, he'll do all right on his own. He's a fighter.'" She reached for a tissue, and I moved the box closer to her. "Please find him."After dabbing her eyes, she added, "I've got money set aside if you need it for the search. I was going to use it to look for him myself, but now ..." Her words lapsed for a beat. "Take it."

My anger at her ebbed. My father might be the same rigid man from my childhood, but my mother had changed—perhaps her illness had done that, or those letters in the attic that had been read and reread.

"Thanks," I said. "I could use it." For exactly what, I still needed to figure out. Before I left the house, I slipped up to Parker's bedroom, found his middle-school yearbook, and tucked it under my arm. It was one place to start.

Chapter 6

My marriage or my son. Where did that put me? I guess I was lucky they hadn't chucked me out on the sidewalk alongside Parker. My brother had warned me, and they'd certainly had enough ammunition.

I've been "odd" as long as I can remember. Parker recognized I was special the December I was five. He was seven and yearned that year for a skateboard, a red one with a diamond-patterned deck. We both snuck into the living room Christmas morning, well before my parents rose. The tree was dark. The lights weren't plugged in at that hour, but the tinsel glittered in the dawn light that filled the room. Parker surveyed the wrapped presents on the floor under the tree, looking for one that might hold his preferred gift. I waited silently, afraid we would get into trouble.

"It's here!" Parker whispered. He picked up a rectangular package and turning, swooped with it through the living room.

I caught his excitement—the vibrations pulsing off him swept over me—and I saw him carving, doing an ollie, even a backflip, each move executed flawlessly, the trundle and smack of the wheels as real as if I were at the park watching him.

When he stopped and returned the box beneath the tree, I applauded. It had been a virtuoso performance.

"How did you do that?" I asked, laughing. Too late, I realized I had spoken at normal volume and clapped a hand over my mouth.

Parker looked at me, puzzled. "What are you talking about?"

"The skateboarding." This time I whispered. "That was fun!" I described what I had seen.

Parker pulled me to the floor, and we sat, crossed-legged, still whispering. "That was my imagination, in my head." He tapped his forehead for emphasis. "QT, you're weird if you could see that."

I wasn't sure what to think. *I was weird?*

He leaned closer to me. "Don't tell Dad."

I nodded in silence. Even at five, I knew it best to keep a low profile around our father, whose allegiance to his faith superseded any devotion to family. As an adult trained to counsel people wrestling with their demons, I've often wondered if my father's rigidity was tied to a deep-seated fear—a fear that his children would turn out exactly as we had.

How do you find someone you haven't seen in more than a dozen years? I started with the email, the cryptic words out of the blue. No, the cryptic words that appeared *after* I'd seen him, conjured him, at Pinscher's. Somehow there was a connection, and I embraced the notion that Parker wanted to be found. The tattered clothing gnawed at my conscience. He needed help, and I had to deliver.

"All of those are excellent suppositions, ladies and gentlemen of the jury," Candi said, yawning theatrically. "But opinion is not a substitute for facts."

We were cycling up the canal path, putting in a few miles of training ahead of the setting sun. Work had kept me too busy to think, but our Wednesday bike rides were my way to reset my emotional calibration. Candi says it's confession and offers me absolution when I've finished unburdening myself. And she's not even Catholic.

Our treat when we're done with the ride is mocha hot chocolate in the winter and iced whipped coffee in the summer. We train year round, not always to race, but rather to be able to enjoy the reward at the end. The one race I never missed was three months away, in mid-June, in Chester County. I had some miles to put in before that happened.

"You want facts?" I said, irritated that Candi was making light of the situation. "Fact 1, Parker emailed me."

"Acknowledged," she said.

The evening was quiet along the canal, so we were able to ride near enough to each other not to shout.

"Fact 2," I continued. "One of Parker's drawings is now a permanent tattoo on my arm."

"That, too, is a fact," Candi said.

"Fact 3, but it really comes before the first two, are the letters from Parker. He wanted me to know he was okay, but now he needs my help."

A dog barked at us as we pedaled past a yard that skirted the canal. A pair of mallards swam to the opposite side bank, blending in with the darkening bushes as the twilight deepened. The air smelled of damp earth and new leaves. It was time to turn and head for the coffee shop before the light failed us altogether.

We were both lost in thought as we sped along the path, the whir of our wheels flicking the occasional stone aside. Inside the warmth of the shop, with steaming mugs of chocolate before us, Candi took the lead at brainstorming.

"Did you try emailing Parker again after your first try bounced?"

I rolled my eyes. "That wouldn't have made any difference. The same thing would have happened." But I wasn't sure. Why hadn't I tried that?

"Do you have any idea where Parker might be living these days? Could he be around here?" She sipped her chocolate thoughtfully. "He last wrote from New York, but he might have returned. This was his home after all."

I shook my head. "He might be anywhere. What's the basis of any URL? The three w's, the worldwide web. That's its advantage and disadvantage. Not many clues to the sender's location unless he tells you."

Candi drummed her fingers on the table. The shop was cozy but filled with the clattering of ceramic mugs and the whoosh and growl of the drink maker behind the counter.

"Who still lives here who knew Parker? You can ask them if they've heard from him, know his whereabouts."

"I'm ahead of you," I said, smiling at beating her to her conclusion. "I grabbed one of his yearbooks from his room. I'll look through it for people he was close to. And I can post a kind of missing person query."

She nodded, still thoughtful. "And that guy he mentioned? Berry?"

Ask Braden for the real story.

"Braden," I said. "A friend of my brother's. He and Parker were…best friends."

Candi and I high-fived, and I was optimistic until she asked, "When was the last time you saw Braden?"

Years. And years. "A while," I said. "But I think his parents are still in the area." At least, last I'd heard.

"OK, good." With that tone, I knew she had switched into organizing mode. If order and planned execution could find someone, Parker didn't have a chance. "What does your inner self say about your brother?"

I sighed, frowning. "Not much." Except for the shimmering image of Parker when I was at the tattoo shop, I had seen and felt nothing. But I'd felt nothing for years. Which meant he was still too far away.

Candi laid her hand on mine and patted it. "Don't worry. You'll know when the time comes."

Just what Pinscher had told me. The room seemed to spin a bit, and I held onto the edge of the table to center myself. The phantom images flickered at the edge of my vision, and I glanced right and then left as I caught the movement.

I pushed up my sleeve to reassure myself the sun was still there, the corona dancing around the solar disk.

Candi gently ran her finger over the tattoo, her touch cool, the sun inert. "It's such an odd thing," she said, "remarkably, wonderfully odd."

I pulled my arm from the table and looked at it more closely. "Yes, it's odd," I agreed. "I could have sworn the prominences were evenly spaced, but now one is missing."

Gail Hewitt kept peanut butter candy in a special tin in her kitchen just for me, for the endless time I spent at Braden's house, following Parker and him around. Chocolate might be heaven, but chocolate and peanut butter are nirvana. She knew my father disapproved of special treats—along with many other things that rubbed his devoutness the wrong way—and she didn't care. "Your father doesn't need to know about these," she explained, as I unwrapped a candy, just the two of us conversing when I was perhaps ten. "Your mother says it's fine, so don't worry." She winked and patted my hand. "Have another to take with you."

I looked up her phone number when I got home from the coffee shop, wiped down my bike, and changed into leggings and sweater. As far as I knew, she and Roy, her husband, now lived on a quiet street in Easton. They had moved shortly after Parker ran away, but my mother had kept in touch.

Mrs. Hewitt answered after three rings. Her voice held the same alto timber I remembered. She laughed when she realized it was me. "Quinn, honey, it's good to hear from you."

We exchanged brief updates. Roy was still active in the local gemstone club, out most Saturdays hunting for minerals in old quarries. She was still teaching third grade, but she had learned how to cut and polish the stones that Mr. Hewitt brought home. "Next time you come over, I'll show you the necklaces I've made," she said.

I fingered the silver owl pendant on the slim chain I wore. Parker had embraced the sun as his symbol, to acknowledge his solstice birthday, and I was swept into the same orbit. For me, though, it was an owl—Quinn means wise in Gaelic. By wearing the owl, I hoped to be imbued with wisdom. It hadn't made much of a difference.

Mrs. Hewitt asked about my parents. I filled her in briefly with the news about my mother. "Oh, the poor thing," she murmured. "And, you, Quinn, how are you holding up?"

I was noncommittal. How do you convey the impending grief, rising like the high tide under a full moon? I reminded myself why I had called.

"What's Braden doing these days?" I asked. Then, because the segue was awkward, I hurriedly threw in, "And how's Tessy?"

Tessy was still working for a major clothing retailer, Mrs. Hewitt said, traveling widely and filling her closet with a dramatically discounted wardrobe.

She lived in northern New Jersey, and was engaged, with a wedding planned for the following year.

I pictured Tessy in an antique lace gown, her hair and makeup perfect. For her, the fairytale she'd dreamed of was actually happening.

"And what about you, Quinn?" Mrs. Hewitt said. "It's been a while since we've talked, but weren't you dating a Brit?"

Jude. The ache in my chest that had dissipated over the last few weeks returned.

"He was from Spain," I corrected her. Although he spoke impeccable English, the flavor that let you know English was not his first language. "It didn't work out."

"I'm sorry, dear," she said. "It's usually for the best."

My heart lurched at that and strongly disagreed.

"And Braden," I cut in. I was not going to reminisce about Jude. "I was thinking about him over the last few days, and realized I've lost track of him. What's he doing? Do you have a phone number for him?"

The line was so quiet I thought the connection was broken.

"Mrs. Hewitt?"

She finally spoke. "He's not well."

<h1 style="text-align:center">Chapter 7</h1>

The most I could get out of Mrs. Hewitt was that Braden had a chronic health issue that had taken a turn for the worse. Even after I told her how critical it was to speak to him—what he might know about Parker could put me on the path to finding my brother—she rang off with only a vague promise to tell Braden I had called. I had no idea where he lived now, but from what little she said, it seemed likely he was somewhere in the area. Could Parker be, too? In a region of nearly seven million people, the odds of finding either of them on my own were pretty slim. Mrs. Hewitt had to come through.

I opened Parker's yearbook and leafed through the pages. If I couldn't find Braden, maybe one of my brother's other pals could help. Several boys and more than a few girls had written gushing phrases stoked with teen melodrama.

Parker, to the laziest summer ever!

You the best, dude!

Never forget what we learned: nobody knows nothin'

I noted the most promising names and started searching for them online. The girls were the least likely to pop up. They'd probably married and changed their name. I sent three of the boys a private message through my social media page, asking them about my brother.

Then I tried one more avenue. I uploaded a copy of Parker's yearbook picture and posted it on my page.

My brother, Parker, as a freshman in high school. He's been missing for several years. Anyone seen him?

I clicked Post. There. I had taken a few more steps toward finding Parker. The sun tat remained quiet on my arm, and feeling like I had done all I could for the moment, I headed for bed.

My mother's first round of treatment was a lie. My father called the next evening to give me the real reason for her medical visit. They met with the neurosurgeon who would attempt to remove the tumor from my mother's brain. If she survived that, with minimal side effects, she might need rounds of follow-up chemo and radiation. The surgery was scheduled for the next week.

"Can you take that day off? You could ride down with your mother and me that morning. It would mean a lot to her to know you were there."

Yes, I could opt out of work, but I felt the walls closing in on me. I'd been out of his life for a decade and my father had not changed. I was still someone he thought he could impose his will on. "I can get away for one day, that's all," I said. I cared about my mother, yes, but I refused to get into a tug of wills with my father.

My father sighed.

"I'm sure she'll be fine," I said, even though I didn't believe that. "You said she liked the surgeon. You're going to the best facility in the area." Optimism can only go so far before it starts to sound fake. "How is Mom today?"

She was struggling with an unrelenting headache and had difficulty keeping food down because of the nausea. My father was worried that she wasn't getting enough calories. It was the nature of the astrocytoma, my research said. That's why it was so vital to remove the tumor—before the symptoms grew worse. But brain surgery was scary even for me to consider. My professional world focused on the mind, a very different part of the head, but no less challenging.

I pulled on my running tights and top and laced my shoes. Twenty minutes of pounding the asphalt around my neighborhood would give me time to decompress from the five demanding patients I'd seen today and the endorphin boost I needed to dilute the sadness about my mother.

When I opened the door of my condo to leave, a man stood there. I nearly slammed it shut, but he said, quickly, "Quinn, wait."

He was maybe thirty, a scruffy beard, hair that needed a comb, and eyes that spoke of the ocean depths, but his jeans and flannel shirt were clean and unrumpled. This wasn't one of my clients, present or past, but he had that hungry look I knew so well. He shifted from one foot to the other, his eyes blinking rapidly. No surprise that the emotion washing over me was nervousness.

I kept the door only slightly ajar, prepared to close it with force if he attempted to push his way in.

"What do you want?" *And how did he know my name?*

"Mom said you wanted to talk to me." I said nothing, trying to fit the words with the fellow standing on my threshold. "It's me, Braden Hewitt."

I tried but failed to hide my astonishment, and opened the door wider. The run could wait.

He stood in the kitchen doorway while I made him coffee and then we sat on the couch in silence for a few moments. My gut said Braden's mysterious illness fell under the substance use heading, which would explain why his mother had been reluctant to talk about him. No one wants to brag about an addict offspring.

"So," I finally spoke, "I apologize for not recognizing you. It's been a long time. Your mom said you hadn't been well. I'm sorry to hear that."

Braden stared into his coffee mug, then transferred his gaze to me. "You heard from Parker, right?"

Astonished again, I blurted, "Do you know where he is?"

Braden shook his head.

"But he contacted you, too?"

A nod of agreement.

Keeping the details brief, I told Braden about the letters, the tattoo, the cryptic email, my mother's request. "I know why Parker ran. And I know you know …" I let my words trail off. "It was my father's doing."

Eyes closed, Braden slumped back on the couch, resting his head on the upper cushion. "We were just kids, Quinn. Parker was wild, I'll give you that, but he was brilliant, so good at drawing. He had a loyal following."

I remembered the sketches he did of family during the holidays. It became a ritual to have Parker draw you—in charcoal, taking only a few minutes to execute, yet capturing your essence. The finished pieces were tacked onto cork board in the kitchen until the evening ended and belongings gathered for the trips home.

Braden sighed. "One day Parker got this idea to draw me, with me as a model. Nude. The way they do it in art classes. And he was good, the renderings were professional, in my eyes, like what I'd seen in the Philly Art Museum on field trips."

Holy cow. If my father ever found those drawings…

"And my dad found them?"

"Yes."

"That must have been ugly."

Braden sat up and put his mug on the coffee table. "I wasn't there, but Parker was crushed." He looked at me again. "That was the end, you know. When your dad threw him out."

I digested this news. "But it was just art, just drawings. He didn't know about you and Parker—"

"He guessed," Braden interrupted. "But we were just kids," he repeated. "It was my fault. I always knew I was different, and Parker, well, I said he was wild, and he was up for it, you know, experimenting. I should have taken the blame, argued with my dad. But by the time I found out about the sketchbook, my mom said I shouldn't contact him, that I was forbidden to come to your house."

So like my father to close off people who no longer fit his idea of what the world should be. But this was family—my brother. The star around which I had orbited since I was old enough to talk.

"I'm so sorry, Braden."

He held up a hand. "I've made peace with it."

I wondered at the truth of that, remembering the hunger I'd seen in his eyes. "And the sketchbook? What happened to it?" I imagined my father tossing it in the fireplace and watching it burn, destroying what he saw as the devil's work.

"Parker left it for me," Braden said. "My mom found it on the porch. He must have snuck it there before he was sent to that boarding school."

"Did you bring it?" I knew the answer even as I asked.

Braden shook his head but smiled, a genuine, gentle smile. "It's safe."

Absentmindedly, I put my hand over the sun on my arm. It was becoming a habit. Almost immediately, an image of Parker took shape, shimmering just behind the couch. The same tattered clothing, his arms reaching out to me. As my eyes widened, Braden looked over his shoulder, apparently trying to follow my gaze.

"What's going on?" he said. "What do you see?"

I bit my lip, the hair rising on the back of my neck. "You'll think I'm crazy. I've been seeing Parker, not a lot, just after the tattoo thing, after finding the letters."

Braden closed his eyes for a moment and when he opened them again, he nodded. "Yes, I've felt this before. It's him."

"But he seems desperate. Do you feel that too?"

The image was fading but like the smile of the Cheshire cat, his face, the hollowed cheeks and penetrating gaze, lingered until the last. *QT*, a voice whispered. The flickers in my peripheral vision danced as well.

"It's like the tattoo has established a connection with him, wherever he is." I wasn't as sure about the flickers. "Can you help me find him?"

Braden ignored my question. "Your dad was tough on you, too."

I shrugged. I too had made peace, at least in that aspect of my past. Who knew what lay ahead, with my mother's illness. "He's a difficult man."

Once Parker's image had dissipated, the room took on an edginess. Braden's right leg was bouncing, and he raked a hand through his hair. He stood up, picked up his mug and carried it to the kitchen. "I've got to go," he said. "About Parker, I want to help you, but I'm not sure I'm up to it."

I gave him a hug. Beneath his shirt, I could feel how skinny he was. He'd been a wiry teen the last time I'd seen him, but this gauntness spoke of pathology. "You can get help yourself, you know," I said. "It's possible to make a fresh start. I see it all the time." The truth, even if the odds were long. Some people made it work. Maybe Braden would, too.

Candi opened her laptop, with me beside her at her kitchen table. Chad was bringing take-out dinner, so we had time before he arrived.

"Where do we start?" I said. We were going to do a deeper dive into the internet to search for Parker.

My post had led to no new leads. Friends had commiserated, offering their condolences and wishing me luck. The former classmates had so far ghosted me.

"I've got a few places to try," Candi said. "Databases that I can access through my credentials."

A few minutes later, she was cursing softly as she tapped the keys and hit Enter time and again. So far, she'd come up with zilch.

"I don't feel so bad," I said, "if *you're* having a hard time finding anything."

She exhaled a sigh. "No results doesn't mean he's not out there. He's definitely under the radar." She entered another search term but still nothing.

I traced the sun tattoo, circling it over and over. "What about sun murals?" I said.

Raising her eyebrows, Candi paused with her fingers on the keyboard. "Maybe." She tried several more searches. "Finally," she said. She clicked on a link.

The headline read, Sun Mural for a New Millennium. I gasped. There is was—the exact duplicate of my tattoo, painted as a mural.

"Where?"

"San Francisco," she said.

I peered over her shoulder and she turned the screen to me to read. It had been painted in 2002, three years ago.

"Ouch," I said, looking at my arm. The tattoo burned fiercely, and, still entranced by the mural image, I rubbed the spot. The flickers in my vision jumped and danced.

The artist behind San Francisco's newest mural says his vision is meant as a salve for the world.

"I'm hurting. We're all still hurting," says the artist, who goes by the alias Whitman's Folly, alluding to what happened last September. "But we're all part of the human race — the sun rises on us all."

I touched the screen to touch his words, as though by that act I could bridge the distance between us in time and space.

"Whitman was his favorite poet," I whispered. "And he's hurting."

Candi turned the laptop around. "Now that we know his alias, and he's hurting. I'll bet we can zero in on him." She did several more searches, and within a few minutes we had uncovered murals by him in Denver, Chicago, Pittsburgh, Boston, and New York—each one of them matching the return addresses on his letters. San Francisco was the only sun mural, but the rest were just as vivid. An Aztec pyramid, a giant scarab beetle, an Egyptian mummy.

"He's good," Candi said. "And weird. A giant scarab?"

I smiled. I didn't care what he had painted. Whatever the subject, it proved he was making his mark. I had enough to try to track him down in person.

My tattoo burned fiercely again for a moment. When I looked at it, another prominence had vanished.

Chapter 8

That week I welcomed Toby's session. Rather than dwell on the big unknowns in my life at that moment, Parker's whereabouts, the meaning of the shifting tattoo, and my mother's health, I could focus on a client—one who I might even say was becoming a favorite. I had to admit, Toby was unpredictable, but counseling had its boundaries and rules, comforting tangibles I could count on. And there was an aspect about him that drew me. Maybe this is what teachers felt like standing before their class. They knew they shouldn't have favorites, but one child ranked above the others—the star pupil. It didn't hurt that Toby was nice to look at.

Instead of sauntering into my office, as he had every time since our first session, Toby bounded in. His energy spilled off him in waves, and he was grinning. I had never seen more than a modest smile before this day.

"Doctor Quinn," he boomed, taking my hand in his and shaking it hard. "I have news."

"A job?"

With that same grin, he told me in rapid-fire cadence about the janitorial post he'd finally landed. He was part of a team that cleaned offices and construction sites. "The pays not bad."

We talked about the challenges he would face now that he was earning money again. His daughter, Eddi, could probably return home from his mother's at some point soon, and he would need to budget to take on her care. Careful money management meant he would put most of whatever he had left into savings. He would have less cash "to burn," money that would be tempting to spend on something illegal.

"I'm so pleased," I said, and with a jolt I realized that I felt more than pleased. I wanted to embrace him, and then feel his arms around me. I quickly buried that thought. He was my client. "You must be happy with what you've accomplished."

Still brimming with energy, Toby blushed. "I am."

"What are you looking forward to the most with the new job?"

He stopped for a moment, pondering. "The chance to be a regular person again." When I raised my eyebrows, he continued. "You know, being able to think about the things that you and other people take for granted, because you're not always wondering where to score."

"Like following the Eagles and Phils? Like seeing your daughter one of these days in a school play?"

His grin was a mile wide. "You bet."

Then his energy dimmed slightly. "I'm also trying to get a friend hired." He looked away from me. "I'm not sure it'll work, though. I think Braden is still using."

"Braden?" My heart slowed. "Hewitt?" The peripheral flickering started up again, and I did my best to ignore it.

Toby's eyes grew rounder. "Yeah. You know him? Does he come here, too?"

I pulled my professional face back into place. "You know I can't discuss other clients," I said, even as I wanted to interrogate Toby for the details. "But I do know of him. I'm not going to lecture you, but I think you're taking a risk by hanging with him."

Toby waved his hands in dismissal. "Acknowledged. But he's a friend. I'll take my chances."

Before I left the office that day, I checked in with Amanda Reed. My plan was to take several long weekends to look for Parker's mural in Boston and, if I hit a dead end there, New York. Candi had agreed to accompany me, her sleuthing hat firmly in place.

"Bad news, Quinn," Amanda Reed said when I explained my request. "With the funding cuts, any time off is going to be unpaid."

When my mouth opened to protest, she held up a hand. "I know. It sucks. I wish it weren't so."

"I've got to go—paid or not," I said. "Family issues. I'll see if Heywood can cover for me."

My mother's offer to finance my search for Parker looked better and better. I wondered if she had told my father. Or was this yet one more secret stirred into the mix of our dysfunctional family?

I kissed my mother and wished her good luck the morning of her surgery. She rested on a portable bed in a pre-op bay, a blue hospital gown bright against the paleness of her face. With a fierce grip on my hand, she whispered, even though my father was nowhere near at that moment. "Is Parker coming?"

"Soon," I lied. If she didn't make it through the surgery, she wouldn't be burdened by knowing that he was still at large. And if she did pull through with her mental faculties still intact, I would explain what had transpired so far.

If you're not a medical professional, I'll spare you the graphic details of a craniotomy. Yes, they do open up the scalp and use a special drill and bone saw to remove part of the skull to get at the brain. The neurosurgeon was to excise as much of the tumor as he could while taking care to disturb as little as possible of my mother's brain tissue. She would be in the hospital for several days afterward, and the medical staff would monitor her for possible side effects. And then she might need chemo or radiation to kill any remaining cancer cells.

That was the hope. An astrocytoma is often fast-growing, so aggressive that it can quickly spread across the brain. So it was more hope than realistic expectation. At least removing the tumor meant that there was less left to treat.

Hour 1. My father paced the waiting room. Fifteen paces down, five across, fifteen up, five across. Repeat. Arms folded as if hugging himself, a hedge against bad news. His brow in a frown. The room was about half full, but the emotional tension surged and vibrated the air. We were all in that cruel limbo of hope and fear.

Hour 2. The pacing continued. I stopped counting his steps, which by then numbered nearly five thousand. I started to read a dog-eared edition of *Philadelphia Magazine*, cover to cover, spending extra time on the glossy ads as a distraction.

Hour 3. I found the hospital cafeteria and bought coffees for my father and me. He refused his, so I handed it off to an older man waiting for his wife, who had a different kind of brain tumor than my mother. My father sat with a blank face, staring at the Bible he'd brought, open in his lap. I wondered idly which verses he'd chosen but didn't peer over his shoulder to find out.

Hour 4. My father dozed in his chair, the Bible closed, the lines on his face finally relaxing. The room emptied, then filled again. Instead of pacing to fill the time, I took a walk around the Penn campus, slipping into a zone of no thought as I ranged over to Locust Walk, to Walnut Street past the bookstore, over to the Penn Museum, the Annenberg Center. Anthrax pounded on my iPod, and I timed my steps to the music. The smell of diesel from the city buses mingled with the scent of fried foods from the food trucks parked along Thirty-Eighth Street.

Hour 5. The neurosurgeon had warned us that the procedure could take up to seven hours. I persuaded my father to get lunch at the cafeteria, and after extracting a promise from the waiting room clerk to find us if there was news, we sat across from each other and picked at our food. My father kept his eyes on his plate. *Did he too wonder where Parker was?*

Hour 6. Forty-five minutes into it, the waiting room clerk called us to a vestibule and told us to sit. The neurosurgeon would be there shortly, to give us an update. My father sat ramrod straight in his chair, silent, his hands folded on the Bible in his lap. He gave off vibrations of anger and fear. I laid my backpack on the floor next to my chair, taking my own emotional temperature. Exhaustion. Worry. Profound sadness. Intellectually, I knew that parents usually preceded their offspring in death, but that fact was small comfort to the psychic rent I felt when I pondered my mother, lying cold in a casket.

Within minutes, the doctor, still wearing his scrubs, his own face lined with weariness, stopped at the doorway to the nook.

"You're the Thomas family?" he asked. When we confirmed that, he perched on the only available chair. "Sonia is in recovery," he said. "The surgery went well."

My father made a small moan. "Thank God," he said, then kissed his Bible.

The knot of tension that had gripped me since morning began to loosen. I reached out and patted his arm. "I'm so glad."

The tumor, the doctor explained, had been sizable, but he was able to remove nearly all of it. It had been a complex surgery because of the tumor's position in the brain, but he didn't think my mother would lose brain function as a result.

We still had several more hours to wait, as my mother awoke from the anesthesia and was moved to the ICU. In the meantime, I checked my father into a nearby hotel, brought his bag up to the room from the car, and insisted he wash up. "It's going to be a long few days, Dad," I said. "You'll feel fresher when you go see Mom."

I wanted to leave him standing in his room and catch the next train home. I owed him nothing.

In the ICU, the nurse in charge of my mother's care told us we could stay for only twenty minutes. I had trouble recognizing my mother. Her face was swollen, and her head was encased in a bandage. My father took her hand gently in his and leaned over to kiss it. How I had longed for that kind of tenderness from him as a child.

I stood on the other side of her bed, taking in the beeping monitor, the drip of the IV line. The emotional air was languid, moving in slow pulses, as she left behind the last remnants of the anesthesia. No pain was wrapped in those pulses. At least she was not hurting physically.

"How are you feeling, dear?" my father said. "They said the surgery was a success."

My mother blinked her eyes several times and looked at my father and then at me. I brought a Styrofoam cup of water to her, and she sipped it greedily. After six hours of intubation, her throat had to feel raw.

She pushed the water cup away, then reached out for my father. She spoke two soft words, urgently, "Where's Parker?"

My father flinched and then went rigid. It might have been in anger or in fear.

Chapter 9

To my father's credit, he did not shout, jerk away, or otherwise further react to my mother's question. He closed his eyes, patted my mother's hand, and murmured a few words I couldn't hear over the steady beep of the heart rate monitor.

Parker is your son, I wanted to scream. I wanted to shake the righteousness out of him. How dare he continue to deny my perfect, beautiful brother a place at the table.

"He's not here, Mom—yet," I said, placing a hand on her shoulder. I knew I was implying that Parker might walk into the room at any moment, but she needed that belief to hold onto. She needed something to live for.

"Stay out of this," my father said. If he could have put up a wall between me and him at that moment, his expression said as much.

"He's part of the family, part of us," I said. I was not going to acquiesce.

"Not anymore, not for years." His tone was dismissive.

My mother began to moan and pull on my father's arms. If she had been stronger, she might have thrashed in the bed. Her reaction must have set off an alarm because a nurse came running.

"Stand back, please," she told my father. She checked my mother carefully.

"I can increase your pain medicine to help you relax," she said, adjusting a knob on a drip bag.

My mother quieted and her eyes closed. Sedation to escape the pain of reality was a path my clients knew well.

The nurse turned to my father. "Whatever happened here made her agitated. She needs to rest to recover."

His lips compressed into a thin line, but he nodded.

"We'll leave," I said. I took hold of my mother's hand and squeezed it. I would find Parker for her. For me.

Candi and I took the Amtrak train to Boston, leaving early on a Friday, a week later. We settled in for the six-hour journey, my hopes high for finally getting a solid clue to where Parker was. And if not that, then a solid grasp of where he'd been.

Candi insisted on paying for her train ticket, leaving me with extra cash for the trip.

"You'll need it," she said as we stood in line at the ticket window. "If not for Boston, then for New York or wherever."

My father had written me a check for five thousand dollars with a furrowed forehead and a down-turned mouth.

"Your mother asked me to give this to you," he said, almost throwing the check at me. "If you had a real job, you wouldn't be hurting for money."

My mother had lied to him about the money's purpose, I realized. A necessary untruth, since I doubted he would have willingly forked over the amount if he knew its real goal. But it still hurt. It was yet another reminder why I'd estranged myself from him. I could never live up to his expectations.

On the train we hashed out our plan for the long weekend. City Hall, the mural itself, Faneuil Market, any leads we found.

By early afternoon, we were climbing the steps from the North Station to street level. City Hall was blocks away but after hours on the train, the walk felt good. I'd called several Boston agencies ahead of our trip but had turned up few details. Maybe in person, I'd be able to do better.

No soaring statue marked Boston's City Hall as William Penn did in Philadelphia. The pudgy building squatted along Congress Street. Inside, I asked directions for the arts & culture office, and we were sent upstairs.

"It's Friday afternoon," the clerk said, when I laid out my request for information on the scarab mural. "Elizabeth is out. She'd be the one to know."

"Can you at least tell us where it's located?" I handed her the printed web page I'd brought from home, the one Candi had found online. "It says Jamaica Plain, but I need a street address. My brother painted it."

The clerk interest perked up. "Your brother? And you don't know where it is?"

Candi interjected. "It's a long story, but no, we don't know where it is specifically."

The clerk studied the page. "A beetle."

"Scarab," I clarified.

"I'll see what I can find." She turned to her computer and a few moments later, wrote something on the page I'd given her. "Found it, just the address. Like I said, Elizabeth might know more but she's not here." She took down my email and promised to leave it for Elizabeth when she returned the following week.

I folded the page with the address and carefully slipped it into my backpack. "Thanks," I said. "This is a big help."

Out on Congress Street, Candi detoured me to a side road and into a tavern. "Lunch first," she said. "I'm starving."

Over burgers and beer, we consulted a tourist map to scope out the address the clerk had given me. The Orange Line on the "T" would get us closest; we could walk the few blocks from there. The small hotel I'd booked us into was on the way. We could check in and hit the mural and return well before dinner.

"We might even have time to visit Quincy Market," Candi said, longing in her voice. "I'm so stoked to shop while we're here."

I couldn't say no. She was doing me a favor by making the trip with me.

We dropped off our bags at the hotel, and hopped on the subway. Emerging on Green Street, we walked toward Centre. Once on the main drag in Jamaica Plain, we studied the building numbers among the shops and cafes.

Within five minutes, I stood outside a small gallery that specialized in miniatures. Right address, no mural.

"Behind it?" Candi suggested. "On the rear of the building?"

I pushed against the front door before realizing that the gallery was closed. "Damn," I said. They would reopen on Saturday morning. We could return the next day to talk to the gallery owner, but I wasn't waiting that long to see the mural. I hadn't traveled three hundred miles to be thwarted by a measly two hundred feet.

"A back alley," I said, and we turned the corner onto a small side street. Yes, an alley opened up almost immediately.

I ran—sprinted—along it to reach the gallery rear, Candi close behind me. The scarab jumped into view, towering over us as we stood in the small lot just behind the building. In bold blacks and grays, the scarab crawled over the sun, its massive size overshadowing the star, its six legs gripping the disc. The effect was imposing in both detail and scope.

I wanted to hold it, to hug it, if only it were three-dimensional. "Parker," I breathed. "He really was here."

Candi walked closer to the wall, peering behind several small bushes that had been planted along the building. "His signature—Whitman's Folly." She held several branches aside so I could see.

My tattoo burned, and I rubbed at it. Did he know I was in this alley, perhaps on the same patch of ground he'd stood on? I felt both elated and discouraged.

"You go on to the hotel if you want," I told Candi. "I want to hang here for a while, soak up what I can of this." And to be honest, I wanted time alone with the mural. Aside from the letters, it was the only physical thing I had of him since he'd left.

"I'll give you half an hour," Candi said. "I'm going to window shop, ask around, and come back for you."

After she disappeared around the corner, I walked to the wall and spread my hand against the cool bricks, over the blackness of the beetle's wing. Gazing up at the mammoth insect, I searched for meaning. The beetle eclipsed the solar disc, holding tight to its edge—and I knew, something or someone had my brother in its grasp and was not letting go. Suddenly sick, I vomited into the weedy bushes at the base of the mural. The sun tat seared the flesh on my arm.

"Quinn!" Candi shouted in my ear. She pulled me from the wall, which I had somehow pushed myself against, as though I were trying to meld with it. "What are you doing?"

I blinked my eyes and wiped a sleeve across my face. I had no memory of what had happened. "The sun, it hurt so much."

She led me to the street. The farther we got from the mural, the clearer my head.

"Tomorrow," I said finally, when we arrived at the subway stop. "We'll visit the gallery when it's open to find out more."

We took the subway to the Haymarket area. At Faneuil Market, we split up. Candi gravitated toward all things Medieval—the more Round Table the better.

I prefer to sift through the detritus as I find it. Drifting past shop after shop, I saw nothing of interest. Discouraged, I was about to go looking for Candi when I heard "Dittohead" by Slayer playing over jury-rigged speakers on a push-cart. "Darkness Reigns" branded the cart's roof. Scanning the shelves, I allowed myself to gape. Tarot cards, black crystals, horned everything. Finally, a place that mattered. I nodded to the seller. "Awesome," I said.

With a happy sigh, I foraged through several shelves' worth of paraphernalia. "What's that?" I asked the seller, pointing to a dinner-plate-sized disk that glimmered slightly from a high shelf.

"Not sure," he said, lifting it down and handing it over. "It was in a batch of stuff I bought from another dealer. Sorry I haven't had a chance to clean it."

The disk was metal, but encased in dirt or clay, as though it had been unearthed after years underground. The glimmer I had seen was from the one edge that the dealer must have wiped off to set it on the shelf.

"Here," he said, giving me a clean rag.

I spent ten minutes removing the grime from the disk. What emerged was a brass plate inscribed with an elliptical circle and circumscribed with graded measuring points. The disk was nowhere near spotless, but I could see enough details to make this something I had to have.

"Five dollars?" I offered.

"Twenty," he countered. "I have a feeling this is something special."

"Eight," I tried. My mistake had been to let him see my genuine interest.

"I've gotta have twenty." Then he turned to another customer.

I plopped the disk on his display table and started to walk away.

"Hey," he called. "Ten. That's it. I can't really go any lower."

When he'd finished with the other customer, I paid him, and he wrapped up the disk. He called it a Tarot plate, but he was making that up. "I decided to give you a break because you cleaned it," he quipped.

I found Candi contemplating a set of swords, waited for her to negotiate a deal, and then offered to buy her dinner, eager to show her my odd purchase.

We took our chances on a nearby outdoor cafe and ordered. She stirred her coffee as I pulled out the disk from my bag. "I found this at a push-cart seller who was playing Slayer."

She rolled her eyes. "Only you would be impressed." Then she sat up, staring at the disk.

Candi took it from my hands carefully, but with a familiarity that surprised me.

"You know what this is, right?"

I shook my head. "It looks Medieval, but history isn't my strong suit."

"It's an astrolabe, for telling time by the position of the stars or the moon." She ran her fingers along the bands, her fingertips pausing at the engraved symbols. "Astrologers used these, too."

I laughed. "The dealer was right. He called it a Tarot plate, but it's probably not worth even the ten dollars I gave him." Parker would have loved it, though. He was crazy for all things tied to the sun and stars. *Will* love it, I corrected myself. "How are you so certain what it is?"

Candi tapped her forehead. "I have an awful lot of trivia tucked away in here. It's nice when I can put some of it to use."

I put the newly named trinket on the table to study as we started on our entrees.

"I used to do the Renaissance Fairs years ago," Candi said. "One of the performers did an act on sextants and these astrolabes."

She briefly described that it was actually a stack of brass circles all set on the large plate called the mater. "One circle is tied to the position of the stars; another circle has the coordinate system — the Earth's latitudes. The mater is the measuring part, kind of like a calculator today."

Candi and I settled down to our dinner, and the frosted brownies afterward. As I licked the crumbs of brownie off my fork, she cleared her throat.

"So what happened at the mural?" she said. "You were almost catatonic, mesmerized."

I shrugged but frowned. The lapse was a blank in my memory.

Candi mirrored my frown. "I must have called your name a dozen times, but you didn't respond until I yelled in your ear."

Then I shivered with a new thought. My mother's diagnosis. Had I inherited it?

Chapter 10

Sleep left me quickly that night—insomnia is my frequent companion even when I'm not wrestling with issues. My mind kept replaying the scarab on the wall, and the troubling blank in my memory.

At four in the morning, I quit tossing in bed. I pulled on running gear and headed out for a jog. Candi snored lightly in the other bed, and I tried not to wake her. The street was still washed in darkness, but the sky was lightening. I jogged toward the docks, this time in silence; no music at that hour. Forty minutes later, I was at the hotel, showered and sipping coffee by the time Candi opened her eyes.

"Impossible that you're awake," she said, yawning. "You are part bat, I think."

"No," I said, "just cursed with a low sleep meter." Along with many other weird things.

After breakfast, we rode the subway out to Jamaica Plain under cloudy skies. The gallery was open by the time we arrived, but Candi stopped me before I pushed at the door.

"Careful," she warned. "No more zoning out."

I shrugged off her arm. "I'll be fine." Now I could get the details I needed.

The gallery owner was a short, plump woman with orange streaks in her dark hair, roughly my age. She vibrated with the slow beats of contentment. The shop itself was a collection of both paintings and craftwork—small fabric wall hangings, small oils and watercolors. All miniatures, as the sign in the window had advertised.

"The mural," I blurted as she turned to greet us. "What do you know about it?"

"The beetle?" She seemed surprised by my question.

"Scarab," Candi and I both said in unison, and all three of us laughed. Briefly, I explained my interest. "Tell me about how the mural came to be."

She smiled and shook her head. "Your curiosity is understandable, but I'm going to disappoint you. It was here when I opened the gallery. I'm pretty new to this block."

My face gave me away because she added, "But I love the mural's weirdness."

I had so counted on finding new details about Parker, but this seemed like a dead end. "Do you know if the former owner paid for its installation or if the city did?"

She shook her head once again. "No idea. I'm sorry I'm no help in your search. It's a marvelous image, though, and I use it in my marketing—you know, big versus little; the giant beetle and the miniature art. I've gotten a great response to that."

Candi paced through the gallery, her face set, and I knew she was deep in thought. I started to thank the woman for her time when Candi turned to her. "Are you sure the former owner didn't leave you any notes about it? It seems like it would be an important part of a real estate deal. It's a public mural."

The woman closed her eyes for a moment, and when she opened them again, she nodded. "Let me look." She disappeared into a back room. She returned with a business envelope in her hand. "You were right. It was tucked into the paperwork from the property transfer." From the envelope, she pulled out a folded sheet of paper, looked at it briefly, and handed it to me. "It's not much."

It was a line of text with a hand-penciled note at the top, "Artist's manifesto." The note said:

And the scarab brought with it the rising sun, the symbol of rebirth.

The typed signature read *W.F. (P.)*

"Yes, this is my brother's," I said, holding the paper reverently. "I'm not sure what the scarab meant to him, but the sun is his symbol." I returned the paper to her. "Is there any way you can make a copy of this?"

"That's the easy part," she said. "I've got a copier in the storeroom. I'll be right back."

I stashed the paper in my backpack and thanked her again. I thought of one more question. "The previous owner. Can I have that name?" They might remember details about Parker.

"I'm delighted that you stopped in," the gallery owner said, copying down the information for me. "I've got the manifesto to share with those interested in the mural, and I can now tell people that I've met the artist's sister." Out on the street, I turned toward the corner without a word.

Come, a thought commanded.

"We're done here, right?" Candi asked.

"Just one more visit," I said. "We're this close." I didn't wait for her to agree, but hurried around the building to the alley. It was vital that I see the scarab again.

She caught up with me as I stood once more before the mural. My sun tat burned again, but I walked to the wall.

"Quinn, no," Candi said. She grabbed my arm. "I might not be able to pull you away this time."

QT, the breeze whispered.

"You don't know," I said to her. "He's here."

"Whatever you have going on in your weird sense, it's just a wall," Candi said. "It's just you and me and the empty lot."

The sun broke through the overcast, drenching us in light, and she was right. We were alone, with only the breeze skittering a few pieces of trash across the asphalt.

We rode in silence on the train to Trenton. I was in my condo by early evening, ready to digest the details I'd gleaned from Boston and begin planning my next scouting trip, to New York.

But my mind would not turn off when I turned out the light. Minutes dragged on with a syrup-like flow, with my eyes wide open, staring into the dimness of my bedroom. I replayed the loop of the giant scarab and Parker's words. *The scarab brings with it the rising sun.* What force had drawn me to the wall?

It seemed like only seconds later that I blinked my eyes open again. I rolled over to look at my alarm clock. Two-thirty in the morning. The loop of thought had ceased, but in its stead, a faint light flashed against my bedroom wall, coming from the hallway. For half a beat I thought it might be Jude. Did he still have a key?

The room was awash in muddled desperation and panic, but it wasn't coming from me. As I stared into the darkness, I heard small taps and thumps from the hallway beyond my bedroom. Too loud to be mice. Muffling the dial tone with my pillow, I dialed 911, but then hung up. Whoever was in the hallway would be able to hear everything I said to emergency response.

I slid quietly out of bed, tiptoed to the door and closed it, pulling a hard-backed chair over to brace against the doorknob. I switched a lamp on low and dialed again. "Someone has broken into my condo," I said softly into the receiver, and gave my name and address.

Still working as quietly as I could, I pulled on sweats and running shoes. I had no weapon, no handgun in my bedside table, nothing to protect me from the intruder but the wooden door separating us. The air will still electric with panic, and in the emotional chaos that vibrated from beneath the door, I knew then who it was.

"Braden," I called out, stepping close to the door, but keeping the chair firmly wedged in place.

A crash beyond the doorway, then a strangled cry of alarm. "Fuck."

In the distance, a siren began to wail, growing closer. *Bless the police.* Although I knew it was Braden, he was likely strung out—why else would he be in my condo in the middle of the night—and he was desperate.

"Quinn," he said. It was a sob more than a word. "I need to talk."

Don't do it, my counselor self shouted. I ignored the warning, pulled the chair away, and turned the doorknob.

Braden pushed through so quickly, I stumbled backward, lost my footing and fell. He lunged on top of me, pinning my arms with his, and pressed a blade to my throat.

"Money," he said, his breath coming in gasps. "Where's your money?"

His eyes darted right, left, anywhere but at mine. The knife pressed harder.

"Stop, Braden." I tried to keep my voice calm, but his panic was unnerving me. "I've got about sixty bucks in my wallet. You can have it, just don't hurt me. It won't go well for you."

Another thump in the hallway distracted Braden enough for me to wrench one arm out from under him and grab his wrist, the hand with the knife, and push it away from my throat.

"No," a voice boomed from the doorway. Someone large and bear-like lifted Braden off me. "This is wrong." I looked up into Toby's face.

"Doctor Quinn," he said, the surprise in his eyes matching mine. He had flung Braden to one side and seized the knife. "I'm so sorry." He knelt to help me sit up.

He started to speak again, but a police officer was in the doorway then.

"Put the knife on the floor," the officer said, his gun drawn. "Stand up slowly and keep your hands where I can see them." He motioned at Braden, still lying on the floor. "You, too. Get up slowly." He kept looking at Toby, whose looming size made him more intimidating than Braden, and pressed a button on the radio draped over his shoulder. "I need backup."

Toby put the knife down and stood, his height and bulk overshadowing the officer. Braden scrambled into a crouch. He pushed a hand through his hair, and I could see him trembling. *Had they planned this together?*

"Up," the officer barked at Braden.

"Braden," Toby said. "Listen to him."

"You, Miss," the officer said, looking at me for the first time. "You called in the break and enter?"

I nodded. "Yes." I felt my neck. The knife had pricked the skin enough to leave blood on my hand. What had I gotten myself into? "But I know these men."

"They're friends? Family? Did you let them in?"

"No. I was asleep and a noise woke me up. That one's an old friend of my brother's, Braden Hewitt. The other one is … an acquaintance, Toby Carson." Ethically, I could not reveal that Toby was my client. He had to be the one to provide that information.

Toby turned to me. "Believe me, Doctor Quinn, I only rode here with Braden because he hit me up for money. When I said no, he said he knew an easy place to get cash and begged me to go with him. I had no idea this was your home. I thought he was going to hit up another friend."

"You were looking for money, too?" What about his new job? Or had he already been fired?

Toby looked down, not at me. "It doesn't look good, does it?"

A second officer arrived in my bedroom doorway. The emotional tide in the room washed over me, almost scalding me with its intensity.

Braden leapt up from his crouch, skittered across the floor, and grabbed the knife that Toby had relinquished. He lunged at me once again, panic in his eyes.

"Halt," the second officer shouted, but Braden kept moving.

"Help me," Braden hissed at me.

The first officer and Toby both moved at the same time to take hold of Braden. There was a scuffle, as the officer seemed to panic, not understanding Toby's intent.

"Shit," Braden cried. In the wrestle for the weapon, Braden had inadvertently stabbed himself in the leg. He crumpled onto the floor, holding his leg and moaning.

Toby straightened and raised his hands, stepping away from the officer.

The second officer radioed for an ambulance, as the first officer put handcuffs on Toby.

I stood up and made a quick self-assessment. Except for the nick from the knife, no physical harm done, but the adrenalin racing through me left me jittery. That Parker's old friend had attacked me rattled me deeply. If Toby hadn't been there to stop Braden…On the other hand, Toby had been there, which meant—what? He was still using?

"Officer," I said, "Toby actually saved me. Braden had the knife."

Braden, still on the floor, holding his leg, glared at me. "I didn't break in. Your door was unlocked. And I wasn't going to hurt you, just scare a few dollars off you."

Remembering the pressure of the blade against my neck, I doubted that. Desperation is a powerful motivator, and the outcome is often not good. Still, I paused. *Had* I left my door unlocked in my distracted thoughts about the Boston trip?

"You're both under arrest for trespassing, possible break and enter, and robbery," the first officer said. "Braden Hewitt, you are also under arrest for assault with intent to commit bodily harm."

Toby sagged with the news. His record would come into play, I knew. Where would that put him on his rehab path? Still, that he had joined Braden in a potential robbery made me shiver. There was much I didn't know about Toby Carson—or Braden.

The EMT crew loaded Braden onto a stretcher and left with the second officer. The first one led Toby down the stairs to the first floor and I followed.

"Can I speak with the lady for just a moment before you take me away?" Toby asked. The officer frowned, but when I nodded that it was okay, he stood a few feet away to give us a bit of privacy.

Despite my misgivings about the evening, I put a hand on Toby's arm out of gratitude. If this bear of a man had not shown up at exactly the right time, I might be one on the stretcher, but with a sheet over my head. "Thanks, Toby."

Toby grimaced. "This was a big mistake on my part." His face settled into a resigned look. "Please don't give up on me."

"I won't." I wasn't sure what had really gone down that night, but I could give him that.

Chapter 11

Telling your boss you've fucked up is never easy. When your boss has held you up as a model for your ambitious co-workers, it becomes excruciating. But I had to do it.

Without alerting the scheduling secretary, I walked in on Amanda at two minutes after nine, two minutes after I had set my briefcase on my desk. Dr. Amanda Reed follows a strict code of ethics and expects no less of her staff.

"Sit," she ordered without looking up. She was sipping Wawa coffee and leafing through a case file. She stopped when she saw my face. "This is serious. Spill."

She flipped from incredulous to irritated and back to incredulous.

"Oh. My. God," she said as I wrapped up relating the events of the evening prior, a mere six hours ago. "You could have been killed." She blew out a breath. "I'm sorry. Of course, you know that. But your client showing up, at your residence, that's not good, Quinn."

I explained that Toby's arrival had nothing to do with me and everything to do with my brother's friend.

"You'll need to turn over your files on Toby Carson as soon as possible," Amanda said. She was already at her computer. "I'll reassign him to Jeremiah, assuming Toby's not reincarcerated. I'll set you up with several new patients. Check with me this afternoon and I'll have their names for you."

"He didn't hurt me," I said, angry that she would jump to that conclusion.

She turned to me and folded her hands on the desk. "It's that attitude that has put you in the spot you're in right now," she said. "We do care about our clients, but our ethics demand that we leave any familiarity at the door. And allowing yourself to feel too much compassion for any of them gives them an advantage. They may or may not act on that advantage. And that may or may not put you in danger. Be very careful of your next steps, Quinn."

Still smarting from the lecture, I made a double espresso in the office kitchen. Too much compassion? Damn it, I did care for Toby, but as I would for any human being who was giving his all, just trying to get through his days clean and sober. That didn't make me a bad counselor or bad person.

Stirring sugar into my coffee, I was so absorbed I didn't hear Jeremiah Heywood come into the kitchen until he almost bumped shoulders with me.

"What's up, Thomas?" He reached up for a mug and looked in mine. *"Double espresso?* No sleep last night?"

I placed my spoon in the sink and yawned. "Too little sleep. Too much chaos."

"Ah," he said. "Chaos. But that's nothing new around here."

In my office, I pulled out Toby's file. I would hand it over to Heywood, but I wished I could find out the real reason he had followed Braden to my place. I'd also promised Toby I wouldn't give up on him. That wasn't violating anything ethical. He'd asked me to do that.

In the file, I looked up Toby's address—and his mother's—and copied them and their phone numbers onto a separate sheet of paper. Just in case they were useful.

I closed the file and set it aside to look at my next client's paperwork. My office phone rang. It was Mrs. Hewitt.

"You called the police on Braden," she said. Not a sprinkle of friendliness. She was not about to offer me a piece of chocolate from her candy jar.

"Hi, Mrs. Hewitt," I said, keeping my tone noncommittal.

"He's badly wounded," she continued as though I hadn't said a word. "The police could have shot him. Because you called them. I had to post his bail to get him released. I can only hope you honor old friends enough not to follow through with the charges."

"What did he tell you?" I doubted Braden would have mentioned the breaking-and-entering, the threats. That's not the kind of news you share with your mother.

"I reached out to him because you asked me to, and now he's hurting." In addition to the anger, I could hear a sniffle. "He only needed a few dollars. He would have paid you back."

I remembered the knife against my throat, the rush of anxiety and panic that flowed from him. "I called the police because someone broke into my apartment. I didn't know it was Braden until after I called."

Mrs. Hewitt laughed, a short bark that held no humor. "Braden rang your bell, and when you didn't answer, he tried the door. It's not his fault that you didn't lock it."

True to form for an addict, spinning a story that casts them as the victim. We work hard in rehab to help them see that.

"At two-thirty in the morning," I said, "I was asleep." True for that night, anyway.

"As I said, he rang your bell."

"I see." Nothing I could say would change her mind at this point.

"I want you to stay away from Braden." She ended the call.

No problem there.

I looked at the paper I'd written Toby's information on. Should I call his mother? I had never met Mary Carson, but Toby pretty much owed her his life. She had found him unconscious after an overdose and called 911. And she had taken in his daughter, Eddi, while he worked to pull his life together. I knew how much that had helped Toby, his understanding that she had his back. So different from Mrs. Hewitt's response. Yes, she had Braden's back but as an enabler.

I sighed, folded the paper and put it in my backpack. Unless he asked me specifically to make the call, I could not reach out to his mother. Once his counselor, I was bound to him even if he wasn't directly under my assistance. After a moment, I realized I could help him in another way. *Don't give up on me*, he'd said. I wouldn't.

I got through my morning schedule on autopilot, not the best approach for a counselor. Two women, one about halfway through the program, the other only a few weeks in.

At lunch, I drove to the police station. I wanted to make whatever case I could in behalf of Toby before diving into any new clients for the afternoon.

At the front desk, I was directed to the clerk's desk, where I explained what had happened the night before. The clerk fiddled with a pen as he sized me up. Jeans, long-sleeved linen shirt, hair as styled as it would allow.

He hit a few keys on his keyboard and looked at the screen, then nodded. "Miss Thomas, it's really up to you on this. If you don't want to press charges, both suspects will be cleared and bail refunded."

"I've thought it over, and I choose not to press charges against either of them."

The clerk nodded again and made a few more keystrokes. "Braden Hewitt was already released on bail. Toby Carson is here in a holding cell. Are you waiting for him?"

"Yeah, if that's allowed."

He directed me to the building lobby and told me to sit tight.

Thirty minutes later, with my lunch break already over, which made me late for an early afternoon client, I was still sitting in the plastic chair. I had seen a parade of people pass by me—officers, citizens, suspects in hand-cuffs—but no Toby.

I went to the clerk to ask how much longer until he was freed.

The clerk checked his computer screen. "Toby Carson was released about ten minutes ago," he said.

"Where is he? I've been sitting in the lobby for more than half an hour."

"Then he probably went out the rear entrance, if you haven't seen him."

Mindful of how late I was running, I jogged around the building to the parking lot. No Toby there either. I couldn't give a ride to an absent friend, so I walked to my car and headed to the office. It was when I was idling at a traffic light that the meaning of what just happened hit me. Toby didn't want me to see him. And that was not a good sign.

I muddled through the rest of the workday. Thankfully, only one client showed, and I could take my time with updating my files.

At the condo, I held my breath as I opened the front door, but there was no sign that anyone had entered while I was away. I'd forgotten to call the locksmith to repair the damage Braden had done to the lock. He had been right in one respect. Although the knob was locked, in my preoccupation with the Boston trip, I had not flipped the deadbolt.

Unpacking my backpack, I laid the slip of paper with Toby's number on the kitchen table. Fuck it, I needed to know he was okay. The number rang several times and switched to voicemail. I shivered. Now he had my phone number. Amanda Reed's words surfaced. *Be very careful of your next steps.*

"Hey, Toby, it's Doctor Quinn." I took a breath. "Just wanted to know that you were okay. Call if you want to talk."

I ended the connection. It really was up to him now.

With a quick sweep of the condo just to make sure there were no surprises, I changed into my leggings and biking shirt, laced on my shoes and did my usual six-mile loop, with Anthrax keeping the pace.

New York kept beckoning. Boston had been kind of a bust. Trying to find the previous owner of the gallery building had proved a dead end. The Big Apple had to give me more solid evidence of where Parker was. My sun tattoo sat inert on my arm, no shimmering images in my vision. Brooklyn, I hoped, would reactivate it.

Chapter 12

"I'm sorry to say, I have some disappointing news," the oncologist said.

My father and I were sitting in the doctor's office at Penn. It had been a month since my mother's brain surgery, and we were there to hear the results of a follow-up test to check for spread of her cancer. True to form, my father had mined my inability to say no by expecting me to take time off from work for the meeting. He both wanted my presence and loathed it—because it made him look weak, that he couldn't handle the issues on his own. He positioned his chair so it was closer to Doctor Wallace than I was. My mother, still weak and prone to falling from the continuing seizures, had stayed at home.

"We'd hoped the surgery would remove most of the tumor, and in my opinion, we did," the oncologist said, his voice confident and assured. "But as you know, cancer is a tricky adversary. The cancer cells can hide out, evading our attempts to eradicate them, and then begin to multiply again. Astrocytomas are particularly aggressive."

"And that's what's happened to my mother?" I asked.

My father's brow was in a deep frown. The spring had been a strain on him, acknowledging that my mother was ill, that he had to turn her over to medical experts, that he could not order her recovery from the leather chair in his den. And, of course, that he had to rely on my help and support.

"Yes," the doctor said. He looked at the paperwork on his desk and shifted in his seat. I felt annoyance vibrate from him. "Studies are showing that a patient's negative attitude—their depression, if you will—plays a larger role in their vulnerability to cancer than we thought—to some kinds of cancer at least. Your mother seems not to care anymore whether she lives or dies."

Doctor Wallace's office contained little beyond the essentials—a desk, three chairs, a computer, and a small filing cabinet. Above the filing cabinet hung a framed photograph of a solar eclipse, at the moment when a brilliant molten gas plume spilled out from behind the moon's disk. I thought of Parker and knew without talking to my mother the reason for her disaffection. Perhaps for the oncologist, the image represented his patients' hidden potential bursting forth after they'd won their battle with cancer.

"I'm sure you're wrong," my father huffed. "Everyone wants to live. My wife is no exception."

I sensed the doctor's annoyance increase. Not only a patient who didn't care, but also a spouse who refused to accept reality. This, I realized, defined their marriage.

"I'd like to start your wife on a round of chemotherapy to help slow the progression of the cancer." He tapped a few keys on his computer. "The front desk will set up the schedule for you. Please stop there on your way out." He stood, ending the appointment.

"How much time will this buy her?" I wanted this out in the open, so my father could not deny it later.

The oncologist's look was direct. "It's hard to predict," he said, and added more gently, "It may not be much."

Time was running out to find my brother. If I wanted to give my mother back her son, I had to make it happen very soon.

I picked up Candi at her apartment that afternoon, and we drove to Philly. After sifting through and rejecting a number of ideas, I had decided the best choice was to visit Pinscher again. He had been both vague and encouraging on my first visit to his shop. I was a conduit, he'd said, but so far the only conducting I seemed capable of was running into dead ends. If Parker was nearby, I needed a spark of some kind to find him. Perhaps Pinscher could give me clearer clues as to how to do that.

"I know how much you want to find Parker," Candi said, as traffic picked up on I-95. The afternoon rush was in full force. "But what if whatever he's mixed up in puts you in danger, too?"

I had already chewed on this, especially since the Boston trip. "What if I don't have a choice?"

Candi was flipping through my radio presets, and stopped at WPRB, the college radio station from Princeton. Appropriately avant-garde rhythms poured out of my speakers and I turned down the sound to hear her. "You always have a choice," she said.

"It's not your brother who's in trouble," I said.

"It was his choice to get involved where he shouldn't," she said.

"You don't know that." I gripped the steering wheel until my knuckles whitened. Maybe I should have come alone. "Besides, I've got this damn tattoo that won't leave me alone. It's a constant reminder. I wished I'd never..."

"Found the letters?" She laughed but quietly. "It's no use wishing for that. But I still say you have a choice. You can walk away and let your brother figure it out on his own, if indeed this isn't all in your head." She patted my knee good-naturedly. "I say that as one friend to another."

"One step at a time," I finally said. "Let's see what Pinscher has to offer."

I parked in a garage at Fourth and Market and we walked the five blocks to the tattoo shop. Except that it wasn't there. I double-checked my phone, where I'd stored the address, and it was correct. The location housed several small storefronts that I didn't remember. Making a random choice, I went into the small clothing boutique with a few draped mannequins in the window. A New U sign hung over the sidewalk. Candi browsed the racks while I asked the proprietor for the tattoo shop's new address.

She looked at me oddly. "We've been here for at least three years. What's the business again?"

When I told her, described the exterior as I remembered it, she shook her head. "Try another street. You must have it wrong."

Candi was already out on the sidewalk, peering into the next set of windows. A barber shop, closed for the day.

"It's not here, but I *know* it was here," I said. With the proof of something else in front of me, though, I felt less sure. "Let's walk up and down a few blocks, ask some other shopkeepers."

We walked a block north and split up, Candi heading east toward Front Street. I walked west. We would text if either of us found the shop. I passed storefront after storefront, but nothing looked familiar, although I did find a tattoo shop. It wasn't Skin Deep, but I figured everyone in the business probably knew their competitors, especially those within walking distance, and went in to ask. I rubbed my sun tattoo for good luck.

Two people sat on chairs in the waiting area, playing games on at their phones. From the back rooms I could hear the buzz of the tattoo needles and the murmur of conversations. A young man whose arms were inked with elaborate whorls of vegetation stepped from one of the rooms to see what I wanted.

"Pinscher?" he repeated when I asked about the missing artist. "I know who he is—at least, I've heard of him—but I've never met him. He has a reputation…" He paused, then stepped closer to the front counter and lowered his voice. "You'll want to watch your step."

I glanced at the waiting patrons, who were still focused on their phones. "What do you mean?" Concern vibrated from the young artist. I massaged my tattoo, which had become warm, almost hot.

"Is that Pinscher's work?" the young man asked.

Turning my forearm up so that the blazing sun was fully visible, I shook my head. "This is why I need to find him."

The man turned away, disappearing into one of the rooms, but returned within moments, trailed by another man around the same age. He too looked at the sun on my arm. "Nice work," he said. "That's not Pinscher's style, though."

Once again I explained that Pinscher was not the artist. "It was Parker Thomas."

The second man's eyes lit up. "I knew I had seen that somewhere."

He knew my brother's artwork? Then I remembered. "The mural in San Francisco."

Enthusiastically, he nodded. "That was awesome. I only saw it online, but wow. A friend sent me the link."

Candi's text lit up my phone with a buzz. *Where r u? Find anything?*

Maybe, I texted. *Give me 5 min.*

"So," I said, addressing both men behind the counter, "Pinscher. Point me in the right direction. Where would I find him?"

The two men glanced at each other. I could feel the concern flowing again from the first artist. The second one spoke. "Try Devil's Half-Acre, near Chestnut and Eighth. Someone there might know."

"Another tattoo shop?" Was I getting handed off to yet another dead-end location?

The first man laughed but with an edge to it. "Worse. It's dark arts."

I waited for Candi to catch up with me, and we headed to Chestnut. She had found nothing tied to Pinscher but bought a blazer at a vintage shop. "Twenty bucks," she said. "It would have been a hundred and twenty new."

We turned the corner onto Chestnut, the sidewalk crowded with people leaving work or waiting outside the cafes and restaurants for friends. A block ahead, in the crosswalk, I spotted Pinscher—I was pretty sure it was him. He strode toward our side of the street and turned to go the same direction we were headed.

"That's him," I said, hurrying my steps. "Pinscher."

Candi craned her neck. "Where?"

"The guy with the ponytail. He's just passing the light stanchion."

She matched my pace, and we pulled near him, only a dozen yards behind. I blinked, and he was gone. What the fuck? We stopped in a shop doorway to reorient ourselves.

"This Pinscher guy is a kindred soul of your brother's," Candi said, scanning the street. "They have an aversion to being found."

We continued up the sidewalk, but more slowly, taking in each shopfront, peering in the display windows. *People don't just vanish.* At the fifth building, the windows were tinted, making it impossible to see through. The sign above the door showed a grinning devil. I pulled open the door and stepped through, Candi right behind me.

The air was still and quiet, unlike the noisy street with city buses, delivery trucks and pedestrian chatter. The emotional temperature of the place was just as subdued. No angst or anger here. Crystals hung from the ceiling in clusters, catching the rays of the lamps and reflecting them into patterns that shifted and moved. The effect was mesmerizing. With effort, I refocused on the clientele. This had to be Pinscher's destination. It fit with the information I'd been given and aligned with the point at which he'd dropped from sight.

"I'm creeped out," Candi whispered, standing at my side. This from a friend who never said no to a dare.

I returned the whisper. "What is it?" I sensed her unease growing but saw nothing that would have triggered it. Books lined several shelves, display cases featured shrunken heads and masks, dried herbs in small packages, and a variety of mortars and pestles. Other items like a full-scale skeleton and witches hats seemed more appropriate for a Halloween costume store. Soft music from a panpipe added a New Age ambiance.

A lone clerk waited on a customer near the rear of the shop. Package in hand, the customer, an older woman with coiffed gray hair, departed, and we were alone.

Ouch. My sun tattoo burned fiercely, making me flinch in pain.

Candi took my other arm and led me to the clerk, who was gesturing to us. He might have been thirty or sixty or ninety. He seemed ageless, serene, and nondescript except for his eyes. Neither blue nor green, but definitely not brown, they carried within them a glow. I looked, looked away, and looked again. I hadn't imagined it. I understood Candi's reaction then.

He smiled a small smile.

"You've come for Pinscher," he said.

Chapter 13

I was about to follow the clerk, who had turned to lead me behind the counter, but Candi tugged on my arm. So dazzled by the clerk's eyes, I had momentarily forgotten she was with me.

"I'll stay out here," she said, her own eyes wide with anxiety. "Be careful."

That she was willing to stay alone in the odd shop, with the odd clerk, told me the depth of her friendship.

"Go find a coffeeshop, a café," I said. "Hang out there. I'll text you when I'm done." I patted her hand. "I'll be fine." I tried to feel fine.

Relief flooded her face, and she fled.

The clerk smiled again. "Ready?"

"I don't need an appointment?"

"He already has you in his books. Come along."

Through a velvet curtain, we walked along a short passage. I heard voices from the room to my right.

"He's almost done with Harrison," the clerk said. "Wait here and he'll see you next."

I stood in the drab hallway and tried to relax. It felt like Candi and I had been on a chase, with a prey that was maddeningly elusive. Or maybe I was making more of this than I should.

The voices grew louder, and Pinscher was shaking hands with a tall, trim man with wavy black hair.

"*Fortes fortuna iuvat*," Pinscher said. The man nodded and left.

When Pinscher's gaze turned to me, my own anxiety dissipated immediately.

"Quinn," he said. "I've been wondering when you would return."

I followed him into his tattoo room and surveyed the table, the shelves and trays with inks and designs. The room was brighter than the hallway but seemed more intimate, warmer. Perhaps it was Pinscher's presence that added that.

"Sit down," he said, pulling out a chair and sitting on another. When I did so, he leaned forward, hands together, fingers intertwined. The crab tattoo seemed to stir, its eye stalks gazing at me. Pinscher's face was impassive. "Tell me," he said.

I almost blurted out my frustration at not finding his shop, but that seemed irrelevant. I was here, he was listening.

"I'm no closer to finding my brother than before," I said. "You said I was a conduit, but I don't know what that means or how that's supposed to help me." I turned my arm over to display the tattoo. "The only thing that's happened is the sun keeps changing. The prominences are disappearing. I'm worried that means he's slipping farther away." I decided to omit mentioning the general weirdness I'd noticed. "And my mother…" I let my words trail off. How could I have thought a tattoo, even this puzzling one that fastened itself to my skin, could have any real meaning?

Pinscher took my hand and arm and examined the tattoo, much as he had on my first visit. "Ah, but it does have meaning," he said.

I blinked. Had I said that aloud?

"Then help me, please." I took a small breath. "My mother is very ill, and she wants to see him before…"

"Of course," he said, running a finger over the sun, tracing the outline and the swirls. Wherever he touched the image, my skin prickled, as though he were a human tattoo needle. The crab danced on his hand. Who or what was this man? Magician? Seer? Tattoo artist was just the surface rendering. When he released my arm, my tattoo seemed almost alive, with a throbbing. I blinked again to clear my vision.

"Your ink is very special. You know that," he said. "It's a rare phenomenon."

So what, I thought. If I couldn't divine its message, its specialness was wasted.

"Let's try this," he said. He flipped a switch on a music player and dimmed the lights. This time, instead of Pinscher humming "Shiny Happy People," the actual REM song filled the room, seeping into every corner. "Put a hand on the sun and close your eyes."

I did as I was told. Under my palm, the tattoo again seemed to be alive. So real the movement felt that I jerked my hand away and opened my eyes.

"Yes, it has power," he said, affirming my unasked question. "And no, I can't explain it. I just know that it is. That's what you must accept as well. Your brother created this image, and through the bond that unites you with him, you unwittingly became a part of it."

The song's refrain beat between us as I pondered his words.

"Then how—"

Pinscher put his hands on mine again. It was an intimate but benign gesture, as though I were in the presence of a greater power. Maybe I was.

"Your brother, he has the same emotional radar as you?"

Emotional radar. I'd never thought of it that way.

"I don't think so," I said. "He knew about it. He helped shield me from my parents—my father. They didn't understand." *They were afraid*, I realized.

Pinscher leaned back in his chair. "Then it was latent in him," he said. He was silent for a few moments, deep in thought. "The rise of Khepri?" he murmured to himself. He looked up at me. "Please try once more. Close your eyes, one hand on the sun."

This time, with the sun growing hot beneath my palm, the darkness behind my eye lids lightened steadily. *QT*, a voice whispered in my ear. Or was it in my head?

Where are you? I wanted to shout.

Here, the voice whispered.

I opened my eyes, and my brother stood just behind Pinscher, and as in my previous vision of him, it was an adult Parker, the one with the hollowed cheeks and piercing gaze.

"Keep your hand on the sun," Pinscher murmured.

"Are you here?" I spoke this aloud, to my brother. He was real yet not quite real. A shimmer around his edges spoke of impermanence.

Yes, the voice whispered. The flickering Parker gave a half smile. *You're all grown up.*

I wanted to jump up, run to him, hug him tightly, but I sat immobile, knowing that if I dropped my hand, he would vanish.

"You are the conduit," Pinscher murmured with a nod. "Do you understand now?"

"Come back," I said. "Mom is…, she wants to see you. I want to see you. It's been so long." Grief built within me, threatening to overflow and sweep me away. What was that saying—so close but so far away? And then the thought hit me. Was this Parker's spirit, his ghost? Was I talking to the dead? I could sense nothing from him, no emotion at all.

I'm alive, QT, the whisper brushed my ear. *But I'm in trouble. Ask Braden for help.*

My mouth agape, I stared at him. "He's fucked up." I felt the knife at my throat, and Toby lifting him away. "Are you mixed up in that?"

No, he whispered. *Not that. But something worse.* His presence strobed. *Much worse.* The song ended and he faded.

"Parker," I cried, but his image was gone. I wiped the tears that streaked down my face. The tattoo had cooled, no longer aflame, but another prominence was missing.

Pinscher cleared his throat, and I looked up.

"Trust in yourself, Quinn," he said, standing and bringing the lights in the room up.

"But how can I save him if I can't find him?"

He put a hand on my shoulder, and a comforting peace streamed into every pore. "Trust what your brother has given to you. Sometimes the puzzle isn't the challenge; it's your view of the pieces."

I walked out of the shop, my head filled with the image of Parker and with Candi's words, You always have a choice. No, I did not.

I met up with Candi two blocks away, at a window table in a small sandwich shop. Settling into the stool opposite hers, I described what had happened with Pinscher and Parker. When the waiter came to take my order, I asked for water. I was buzzed enough with adrenaline—no need for caffeine.

"He was there, in the room, but he's in trouble," I sighed. I felt a deep ache in my chest. "We've got to try New York, find him."

Candi sipped her coffee, watching me. The anxiety that had poured off her in the dark arts shop was gone, replaced with something else—envy?

"It's so frustrating," I said. "And all Pinscher did was tell me again to trust myself."

Still Candi said nothing. The silence grew awkward. Finally, after the waiter had refilled her mug, she spoke.

"If I had your super-power, I wouldn't be complaining," she said. "Make it work for you. Use it to find him. Or shut up about it."

It was my turn to sit in silence. Inside, I seethed. "You don't know what it's like," I said at last.

"No?" she cocked an eyebrow. "How could I not? It seems like all you ever talk about." She stirred her coffee, clinking the spoon sharply against the mug. "We're all special in some way, but you forget that."

It wasn't envy that I sensed from her anymore. She sent out sparks of anger. I contemplated the change in my friend. Always one of the first to laugh at a situation, she had kept me centered over the years, tempering my seriousness with her levity.

"I never said—"

She cut me off. "But you meant it." She sighed, running a hand through her cropped hair. "I'm tired of it, Quinn. I do want to help you, but it just gets old."

She looked out the café window, watching the people passing. I saw the glisten in her eyes.

"What's this really about?" I said, gently. "You're angry, but you're also steeped in sadness. What's happened?"

The fierceness of her gaze made me recoil. "That's the other thing," she snapped. "Stop reading my feelings. They're none of your business." Abruptly, she looked down, staring into her mug.

"Isn't that what friends are for?" I said evenly. "To help bridge that gulf between being at sea with your emotions and the sureness of the shore?"

"It's just not fair," she said, and two tears trickled down her cheeks.

Echoing Pinscher's earlier command, I said, "Tell me."

"Chad," she said. She dug for a tissue in her bag. "He's done, called it quits. He's now my ex." She dabbed at her eyes with the tissue and looked at her phone. "As of seventeen minutes ago."

"Jeez, that sucks," I said. "I'm so sorry." I thought of Chad's werewolf tattoo, the man transforming under a full moon. Unfortunately for Candi, the wolf had won.

Chapter 14

My couch wasn't a place where I would want to spend a lot of time sleeping, but Candi said she didn't mind. It was only for a few days, she said. Until Chad moved his stuff out.

"You could always put his junk out on the front lawn," I suggested.

She made a face. "Too much work. But I did give him a deadline. If he's not out by next weekend, I'll call in a few people who owe me favors to give his stuff the boot."

I was glad I had paid for an extra deadbolt for my door. Braden's brazen entry into my apartment would not be repeated. He didn't have a key to the new lock. I felt safer for both Candi and me with it in place.

The next morning, I got up early for a run while Candi got ready for work. She's a rotating librarian, traveling to a different branch several times a week. My first client wasn't scheduled until nine thirty.

As I stretched at the front railing of the building, Judas Priest's "Breaking the Law" queued up in my ear buds, the sun tattoo remained quiet. No changes, no warmth. No hint of what had happened the day before. Pinscher had told me to trust myself. I wasn't sure I could.

At the office, I pulled out my iPod from my backpack and a slip of paper fell to the floor. Toby's phone number and his mother's. He hadn't returned my earlier call. With a good thirty minutes before my first client, I called him again. When the call switched to voicemail, I hung up. I hadn't talked to him since that night in my condo, and I still wanted to know what was going on. Poised to dial his mother's number, I decided instead to mosey to Heywood's office and ask him for an update on Toby.

"Carson?" Heywood said, flipping through his folders and pulling out the one I had handed over when Amanda removed me as his counselor.

"Yes, he was doing well the last time I saw him," I said, leaning in the doorway, crossing my arms.

Heywood leafed through the pages—my pages—and then looked up. "He's missed his last few sessions without canceling. I wondered why the name didn't register. I haven't seen him yet."

"Damn," I muttered.

Heywood waved a finger at me. "Thou shalt not get involved with clients," he said, but grinned. "However, there are no rules against getting involved with the staff."

"That's not it, Hey," I said. "He's someone I felt a real connection to, but it's totally professional." I turned to leave but waggled a finger back at him. "Professional for you, too." Heywood was more a sibling than ever a love interest.

"I can always dream," he said, more than a little rueful.

In my office, I kept thinking about Toby. An addict who ghosts a friend springing them from jail and then blows off a number of counseling sessions likely had been lured back by their old demons. He'd been so close to moving on to a new stage in his life—his daughter returned to him, a steady job to build a new foundation for his life.

Late in the afternoon, on a break, I phoned Mrs. Carson.

"He didn't call you?" she said. She sounded surprised. "He told me what you did—thank you. He's got the day off. Just a minute—" The phone sounds were muffled.

Toby was on the line. "Doctor Quinn," he said.

Startled and relieved, I blurted out, "How is today?" It was our standard opening line for a session, and all I could think of quickly. I tensed, waiting to gauge his answer. Phone lines do not transmit emotions for me.

He chuckled. "Today is a five."

I blew out a sigh. "I've been worried. It's been a while."

"Understandable."

I could hear Mrs. Carson say something in the background, and a young child laughed.

"I know you can't be my counselor anymore. The center let me know. I screwed that up—"

"No," I said, interrupting. "You saved my life. I owe you big time."

"Braden is..." he started, then paused.

"Not your responsibility," I said.

"But I should have known."

"You didn't. Let's set the topic of Braden aside for now. How's Eddi?" My office clock said I had five minutes before my next client showed up.

"Fine," he said.

"I'm glad to hear." I measured what to say next. He mattered to me. I so wanted him to succeed.

"Can you come to dinner tonight?" he said. "My mom makes a mean chicken diablo, and she would be happy to show that off. And you can meet Eddi."

Once more I was surprised and tongue-tied for a moment. Not what a counselor should be. I weighed the options. I was skating close to crossing the line ethically, but dinner with his family seemed benign.

"That's sweet of you to ask," I said. "I would enjoy meeting your family."

He made sure I had the address, we settled on a time, and I hung up with a minute to spare before my next appointment.

Mary Carson lived on a quiet street in Bensalem, the block's maple trees creating a canopy over the roadside. I parked in front of the house and picked up my dinner contribution, a loaf of bread from an upscale supermarket. I felt a twinge of guilt at leaving Candi on her own that evening, with her breakup with Chad still so raw. But bringing Candi along would have been unethical as well as awkward. I wasn't sure how the evening would go. This was uncharted territory for me.

A young girl with brown pigtails and a Hello Kitty T-shirt pulled open the door to greet me when I rang the bell. She stared at me, eyes wide. Toby's bear of a form showed up behind her, scooped her up, and opened the outer glass door.

"It's Doctor Quinn," he said to the girl. "Let's let her in, okay?"

The girl nodded, still staring at me. She sent out waves of curiosity tinged with anxiety. A youngster's emotional flow is so pure, much different from the complex vibrations that adults send out—or the muddled chaos of someone high or drunk.

"Hi," I said brightly, hoping this was the right approach. "You must be Eddi."

As I passed by Toby and Eddi, she reached out and patted my shoulder. Toby winked at me.

Mrs. Carson swept into the living room, where we stood. "Ms. Thomas," she said, taking my hand in both of hers. "We are so happy to have you for dinner. I hope you like lemonade, I've made a fresh batch." She stood a head shorter than her son, but still tall. Her dark eyes were friendly behind her glasses. Like Eddi, she gave off a wave of curiosity. "I'll get you a glass. Dinner's almost ready."

Toby sat on the couch, with Eddi on his lap, nestled into an armpit. She still watched me, silent. I chose a green stuffed chair by the front window. I heard clinking from the kitchen and smelled frying chicken.

I waited for Toby to speak, but he seemed more intent on Eddi, most likely as a deflection of what I needed to know. After a few more moments of quiet, I plunged in. "How are things?" This was a delicate line to walk, with his daughter in the room. She was too young to understand, but she would pick up on the underlying emotion.

"Fine," he said, but he would not meet my eye. I could feel an anxiousness replace the calm that had first greeted me.

"Daddy," Eddi said. She squirmed out of his arms. "I'm going to help Mom-mom." With a last wiggle off Toby's lap, she padded barefoot around the corner to the kitchen.

"Wow," I said, "she's pretty independent at what three, four?"

"Four." He still wasn't looking directly at me. "Yeah, she's quite a kid."

"Toby." I let the name drift as he shifted his position on the couch several times. "I think I know the answer to the question I'm not asking." When he still did not respond, I continued. "Just to be clear, I am here as your friend. I'm not here in an official capacity. And as a friend, I care about what happens to you."

Finally, a nod from him. "I'm fighting it," he said softly. "I don't want to get sucked back in."

"Good." His flow of emotions gave no hint of using, and I relaxed slightly. "That's a great start. What's your plan?"

But Toby was spared answering because Mary reappeared. "Dinner's done. Eddi's already at the table. Come and get it."

Whatever Toby might have said never resurfaced. Instead, we chatted about the spring weather, Eddi's days in preschool, and Mary's backyard garden, already producing lettuces and herbs for the season. The chicken was tangy and tender, the salad of fresh greens expertly dressed, and the lemonade a perfect blend of sweet and tang. Eddi ate enthusiastically, adding a comment now and then directed at Mary or Toby. I enjoyed the closeness I felt around the table and relaxed. Toby had a solid support system in place.

After clearing the table, we moved to the living room for coffee. Mary seemed to sense the need for Toby and me to have a private conversation, because she hurried Eddi off to an early bedtime. Eddi approached me to say good night and patted my knee.

"Are you going to be my new mommy?" she said, eyes searching my face.

Flummoxed, I tried to keep a neutral, friendly face. "I'm a friend of your daddy's, sweetheart. We're good friends."

Mary laughed and guided Eddi out of the room. "That's right, pumpkin. Let's leave these two friends alone."

Once again, I sat opposite Toby—he on the couch, me in the stuffed chair. Maybe this had been a mistake, coming here. I could let it go, but I didn't want to. My tattoo had been doing a slow burn since dinner, and I rubbed it.

"So," I started, then the doorbell rang. I swore under my breath. Yet another interruption in a conversation I needed to have.

Toby went to answer the door, and I pondered my next steps.

A scuffle at the door, and Braden burst into the room, Toby restraining him by the shoulder.

"No, you have to leave," Toby said. "I can't have you in my mother's home."

Braden stopped moving when he saw me, but Toby kept one hand on him. Wise move, I thought.

Standing quickly, to be on the same footing, I faced him. "What are you doing here?" I tried to sound fierce and no-nonsense, but inside I quavered. He wasn't carrying a knife, but maybe he had one stashed in a pocket—or worse, he had a handgun.

"I followed you," Braden said. He tried to jerk his shoulder free from Toby, but Toby's hand was like an iron clamp.

"I've been here for more than hour," I said. "How is that possible?"

Braden shrugged. "So, I've been sitting in my car. I got tired of waiting for you when you didn't come out."

Toby turned Braden around and pushed him onto the couch. "What do you want with Doctor Quinn? You've already caused her—and me—enough worry."

With one knee jittering, Braden glanced around the room. "Your mom's?"

"That's what I said. I also said you can't be here." Toby balanced on his toes, knees bent, hands at his sides. He had the bouncer moves down, I thought. "I'll give you about five seconds to answer me, and then you're going to leave."

Braden held up his hands. "I just wanted to tell Quinn thank you."

"For that, you follow her, force your way into the house?" Toby voice dropped to a growl. Eddi was just up the stairs, and so was his mother. If Braden could hold a knife to my throat, he could do the same or worse to Toby's family.

I gathered my bag. "You're welcome," I said. "I'm heading home now. But I don't suggest you try my front door. I gave you a pass on your last visit. That was a one-time occurrence."

When Braden tried to rise from the couch, Toby pushed him against the cushions. "I'm going to wait until Ms. Thomas is gone, then I'll escort you to your car."

Grateful, I put my hand on Toby's arm. "Thanks," I said. "Please thank your mom for dinner."

"Quinn," Braden said as I opened the front door. "I wanted to let you know something."

I turned to look at him. His knee jittered more quickly now. The longing that poured off him told me he was badly in need of a chemical something.

His fixed his dark eyes on me. "I know where Parker is."

Chapter 15

Through my childhood and into my teen years, Parker often asked me about my weird sense—probing, listening, almost with a wistfulness. "You're special," he said when I was eleven, and he was thirteen. "What you've got is very cool. Don't ever let anyone make you feel bad about that."

By "anyone," I knew he meant our father.

We were riding skateboards in the parking lot of the empty softball field two streets over from our house, waiting for Braden to join us.

By that age, I no longer regularly saw images when I picked up on others' emotions. That had faded with time or maturity. But the vibrations had grown stronger and more distinct. They divided tonally into distinct bands of sound apparent only to me. Fear was high pitched, a rapid pulsing; joy and pleasure were lower, slower—like a good stretch after a long bike ride.

When I turned thirteen to Parker's fifteen, we were part of a tribe of three—Parker, Braden Hewitt, and me. Tessy, Braden's older sister, wanted little to do with us. She ran with a different crowd and was almost done with high school.

I loved Braden by extension. He was Parker's best friend, and because we lived only three doors apart, I saw him often. Parker and Braden stood about the same height, an inch taller than me and I was tall for my age. But Parker's dark wavy hair contrasted with Braden's short, sandy locks. Parker's eyes were brown like mine, Braden's were blue. Both were slender and athletic. Both ran cross-country on the school track team.

As the next year slipped by, I felt a change in Parker. More times than not, he and Braden were busy with their own projects, and I was gently excluded.

One late afternoon, when our mother was out running an errand and our father was still at work, Parker came home, his face flushed, a smile on his face and in his eyes. He had walked into the kitchen for a snack and didn't notice me.

"You're in love," I said aloud, in wonder, finally identifying the emotion I had been picking up.

His face immediately closed, and the vibrations switched to panic.

"Who says?" he said.

I smiled, hoping to bring back his lighthearted mood. "No one's here. It's just us."

He looked around as if trying to confirm my words, his eyes still wary. "Why do you want to know?"

I moved closer to him. "Because I'm your sister, and I'm happy you're happy." I paused. "It's Braden, isn't it?"

His mouth turned up in a small smile. "Yes."

"Wow," I said, surprised but not surprised. "Cool."

"It's the best feeling," he said, his eyes lighting up again. "Someday you'll know."

We both flinched as we heard the garage door opening. Our mother had returned from her errand.

I raised a finger to my lips. "I won't say a word. It's our secret."

But, of course, secrets can be broken. I kept my promise, but someone else must have ratted on them. One night, my brother slammed his door, and through the wall that separated our bedrooms I heard him crying. There had been an argument, raised voices in our father's study. I was not invited to participate.

Very early the next morning, I was awake at dawn, troubled by the despair that flowed from his room to mine. He crept into my room, closed the door and sat on my bed, checking that I was no longer asleep.

"They're sending me away," he whispered. I sat up in bed. "Where?" I knew the why without having to ask.

"A boarding school. As far from … from here as they can send me, I guess." He was angry and sad. "I'm sixteen! Nearly grown up. I'll run away."

"They'll bring you back."

He looked at me fiercely. "Not if they can't find me." His eyes glittered with tears. "And they can't keep Braden and me apart. I'll find a way."

I wanted to say, "But I'll miss you. Don't go." Instead, I felt my own eyes tear up. If he stayed, he would suffer. If he left, I would just have to hope I would see him again.

"This is our secret, QT. They'll tell you that the boarding school was a recommendation from the principal, some bullshit about what's best for me. But you'll know the truth. Just don't let them know you know."

"Why not?" I was shaking now.

"Because you might get the boot, too. We're both the weird ones in the family. You with your odd sense and me with my … my 'immoral attractions.'" He rubbed an arm across his eyes. "I'll come back somehow."

And so my brother packed up, went off to the boarding school—but never returned. And I kept his secret, swallowing my parents' explanation like the good daughter I pretended to be. But once I turned eighteen, I didn't set foot in their house again.

In my car, against my better judgment, I faced down Braden. We couldn't have this conversation in Mrs. Carson's home. It wasn't her business and having Braden there put her at risk. I didn't want this conversation in Braden's car. I would feel trapped, and that was a primary tenet of addiction counseling. Never put yourself in a position of vulnerability.

So it was my car, and we would play by my rules. Toby sat in the back seat. His presence made me relax a bit. I could trust him, I thought.

Then he spoke up. "Would you mind telling me what's going on? Who's Parker?"

Braden's knee had resumed its bounce, which made the owl ornament hanging from my rearview mirror jiggle. "Her brother," Braden said.

I sighed, turning to Toby. "He's been gone for a long time. Braden knows him from way back." I studied Braden. Panic and anxiety were vibrating off him. I wondered at the announcement he'd made in the house. "You've already said he'd contacted you. What's changed?"

"I hated your dad," Braden said. In the dusk, his face was beginning to fade into darkness. His tone was bitter. "He ruined what we had, me and Parker."

"I agree," I said. "Parker fled, and you escaped in your own way. Now your escape plan has you by the balls."

"Yeah," he said. "I've always thought you could have done something to stop what happened. Put your mind-reading to good use."

"It's not mind-reading," I said. This assumption was a prime reason I didn't discuss my emotion radar—as Pinscher had characterized it—with anyone, with very few exceptions.

"I'm not following you, Doctor Quinn," Toby said.

"You know how you can sometimes tell a person's emotions by their body language or their facial expression? I can go deeper. I can zero in on those emotions, but it's not mind-reading. I don't know your—or anyone's—exact thoughts."

"You use it in your work," Toby said. It was a statement, not an accusation. He had grasped the idea quickly.

"Yes," I said. "It gives me an 'in' with my clients, a tool to help me help them." Toby also didn't need to know my life-long struggle with the sense, the question that always lurked just beneath the surface. Was I blessed or cursed? Or was I just plain weird?

"Cool," Toby said.

I relaxed slightly, glad that Toby wasn't upset about my sense. "Braden, I was only fourteen. I was powerless."

Braden was silent, his knee still jiggling. I could no longer see his face. Panic streamed from him, plus a raw, savage longing—the emotion of the addict out of control. I felt the first pinprick of fear inside me. My tattoo seared my arm. He was too close and too unpredictable. I regretted that I had allowed him into my car.

"But now you've stirred it all up again," Braden said. "Why?"

"I told you the last time we met—I have to find him. He's in trouble."

"You can't," he said. It was a strangled cry, and he lunged at me, a knife glinting briefly in the light from a streetlamp. Toby's beefy arms moved at the same time, pinning Braden to the seat. I opened the driver's side door and jumped out of the car.

"Fuck!" Toby yelled, and Braden opened the passenger side door. He ran to his car and roared off.

A low moan brought my attention to Toby. Leaning in the door, I could see him holding his left arm with the other hand. In the glare of the dome light, the blood seeping through his fingers looked black.

"The sonofabitch stabbed me," Toby said. Pain came off him in waves.

"You need the ER," I said. "Is Saint Luke's the closest?"

Five minutes later, I dropped Toby off at the emergency department and parked the car. My mind churned, trying to fit the pieces together. Toby and Braden and Parker. Were they connected? Yes and no. Did it matter?

Inside the hospital, I was directed to the emergency bay where Toby rested, his face pale with pain. A doctor not much older than I stitched up Toby's left bicep.

"You are family?" the doctor asked.

"She's cool," Toby said.

"Mr. Carson has declined pain medication," the doctor said. His name tag said "Dr. McManus." "But he did allow us to numb the wound area to apply the sutures."

"How bad is it?" I moved next to Toby, opposite the doctor.

"He's suffered a deep laceration to the left bicep. We've cleaned the wound, and I'm closing it with self-dissolving sutures." McManus worked quickly, precisely, calmly. "Mr. Carson says he was stabbed. Has this been reported to the police?"

"No," I said. "Not yet. We were in a car when it happened, and I drove here immediately afterward. I was worried about the amount of blood."

McManus finished suturing and stepped aside to let the nurse apply the sterile covering. "He'll be fine. Not that much blood loss, but the knife may have injured the muscle." He tapped at the keyboard on a small computer. "Mr. Carson, I'm giving you a prescription for antibiotics. Are you sure you don't want a script for pain, as well?"

"No, I'll be okay," Toby said.

"You're tough." I took his hand and squeezed it.

McManus studied Toby for a moment, then caught my eye and nodded. He understood the situation. "Try over-the-counter ibuprofen to ease the swelling and inflammation. Keep the wound clean, and it should heal in about ten days. And," he added, "there's a police officer in the emergency lobby if you want to report the incident."

With Toby in a wheelchair, we sought out the officer. Even if he was an old friend, Braden had assaulted Toby. I couldn't give him a pass this time. It wasn't my injury. And I had been his intended target. What was it that Braden wanted?

The officer directed us to the police station, where we both gave our statements. What I couldn't provide them with was Braden's address, since I doubted he was still staying with his parents. I was spooked that he had followed me to Toby's. I texted Candi to remind her to lock the deadbolt on the condo's door.

At Mary Carson's house, we sat for a few moments in the car. Toby planned to stay overnight at his mother's, and then try to work the following day.

"Thanks, Doctor Quinn," he said.

"The thanks should be from me to you — if you hadn't grabbed Braden …" That knife would have punctured something vital. I shivered.

He leaned close and brushed his lips across my cheek. "Quinn," he said softly. He got out of the car but turned to say, "Be careful."

What had I gotten myself into? Toby's gesture was sweet, but ethically, we could not become romantically involved. He would always be my client on some level.

The sweetness of Toby's kiss melted away when I arrived at my condo. Alarmed by Braden's attack, I scanned the parking lot and shined a flashlight in the bushes on either side of the steps leading to my door. Once safely inside, I locked the deadbolt.

Candi was just settling in on the couch, so I quickly filled her in on the evening's events. It was her turn to shiver.

"No kidding, be careful," she said, then yawned. "Sorry, I've got an early meeting at the library in the morning. We're safe enough here, with the doors locked. He's an addict, not a professional assassin." She immediately added, "I'm mean, he's your friend. No disrespect."

"Candi, he's tried to hurt me twice." I opened up my laptop to check emails. I was still too keyed up to sleep. "You can disrespect him all you want."

I had two messages waiting for me, both from the classmates I had reached out to, asking about Parker. The first was brief.

I haven't seen him, but I heard he was mixed up in some cult with a weird name, like capri.

The other went on for several paragraphs, but the gist was similar. Parker had fallen in with a group of people who worshiped the sun. *So like him,* I thought. So like the brother I knew, I corrected myself. He sought out the path least taken, no matter the consequences.

Candi was asleep by the time I made the rounds of the condo, checking every last window to make sure they were locked.

<h1 style="text-align:center">Chapter 16</h1>

Hoping to avoid Amanda Reed the next morning, I let myself in the side door to the building and hurried to my office, head down. My first client was due at half past ten, which gave me time to catch up on my reports, something I knew Amanda would be asking about much too soon.

In the lunchroom, I poured a mug of the brewed house brand we had to put up with and added a spot of milk. Then Amanda pounced, slipping into the room while my back was turned.

"Quinn, I've been looking for you," she said, her no-nonsense face on full display. She frowned briefly and started to say something, but seemed to change her mind. "Five minutes, my office, please." She didn't stay for my acknowledgment. Probably on her way to fire a salvo at another counselor.

Just shy of five minutes put me in a chair opposite her. "I've got a client due in about fifteen minutes," I said, making a show of looking at my watch.

"Twenty," she corrected. "What I have to say won't take more than five." She sat and studied me. I picked up annoyance, irritation—nothing new coming from her. Finally, she sighed. "Quinn, you are one of the best counselors in this office."

She let that sit while she shifted some papers on her desk. I savored the morsel of praise because it knew it would soon be swept away.

"But," she continued, "you have stopped pulling your own weight. I'm not going to psychoanalyze you to find out why, but I suggest you rethink your priorities." She cocked her head, awaiting my reply.

What could I say? That my mother was dying of cancer? That an old friend had almost fatally stabbed me? That my long-lost brother might be trapped in a cult?

"I've had a lot on my mind," I said.

She raised an eyebrow. "I see. And is Toby Carson one of those things on your mind?"

Toby? I fumbled for words. "Uh, no. He's Jeremiah's now." Damn Heywood. He must have shared his speculation with her.

"Do I need to remind you that a counselor keeps her personal life distinct from her professional life?"

I shook my head. Amanda was winding up to full-blown lecture mode.

"I'm not going to scold you, Quinn. I'll just say, crossing that line can be dangerous."

I thought of Toby's stab wound. A knife was an incredibly easy weapon to hide and almost impossible to protect yourself against.

"Just think about it," Amanda said. "I don't want to lose you."

Amanda was right, of course. I had let my personal life interfere with my client work and that client work was vital to my well being. If my emotional radar, as Pinscher had put it, was my fate, then putting it to use to help people in recovery made me feel less like a freak. I was a counselor, a good counselor, and part of that success could be tied directly to my ability to sense accurately how a client was feeling.

That morning I poured myself into my work, saw two clients back to back, and felt like I had helped each one move a bit farther along the path to normalcy.

Toby got a call through to me after the second client to tell me his boss had let him take several days off to heal.

"I didn't think he would believe me," Toby said, sounding surprised. "But he did."

"He trusts you," I said. "You're building a solid footing. I'm sure it feels good." It was an important step back into the real world. "How's the arm?"

"Sore, but I'll live. I've had worse thrown at me."

We chatted about his daughter, his mother, the job. Then he asked casually, "Can I see you again?"

I took a deep breath, remembering that brush of a kiss. "Of course, and any time. You're still my client, and I care about you. I'll always be here for you, but as much as I like you, we can't move our friendship to the next level. It wouldn't be ethical."

There was a pause. "I'll take just your friendship," he finally said.

"I'd love that," I said. "But it's absolutely your choice."

"Done," he said. "So, how can I help you find Parker?"

I begged around the office—mostly Heywood—and freed my Friday of that week to make the trip to New York for more digging into Parker's past. I still had the money from my mother, especially useful since once again I would not get paid for taking a day off. Toby was onboard with the trip, and

Candi, although she griped on the phone, arranged for another day off to accompany me as well.

Unlike Boston, New York kept no record of murals that weren't officially sanctioned. Candi's research had unearthed nothing about his mural there beyond a photo and caption that ran shortly after it was finished. When we started up I-95 for the city, we had a neighborhood in Brooklyn as a destination and little else. Maybe I would get lucky as I had with the scarab at the Boston art gallery.

"How will seeing the mural in person help you find your brother?" Toby said from the back seat.

Candi snorted in laughter. She was riding shotgun. "It's Quinn's belief that doing the in-person thing will magically conjure him up."

My face grew warm. She wasn't far off even if she was joking. "I know it's silly to think that, but I have to try something. The murals are physical evidence of my brother. The other leads are just rumors for now."

"And the last mural almost sucked you in," Candi said. "Is that why Toby's along, because he's bigger and stronger than me? A better rescuer?"

Ouch. "Yes," I admitted. "An extra measure of security can't hurt."

Toby chuckled. "If it's strength you need, you've got it. I can't do much about the magic part."

We took the Verrazzano bridge as a way to avoid driving white-knuckled through Manhattan, and parked on Dekalb Avenue in Fort Greene, a street in the general area I thought the mural might be.

We decided to split up but stay in touch via phone and reconvene in two hours for lunch—unless one of us hit on a clue before that time. We'd picked a commercial street to make it easier to connect with people. I didn't relish knocking on strangers' doors in a city I didn't live in. Businesses would have to allow us inside, and once there, we had to get lucky. Candi's research had confirmed the mural was somewhere there.

With a deep breath to steel myself, I pushed open the door to a neighborhood hardware store and threaded my way past garden hoses, electrical supplies, and hammers to the register. Three people stood in line to check out, and I took position behind the third.

When it was finally my turn, I held up the photo of Parker's Aztec mural that Candi had printed out from the website.

"I'm trying to locate this mural," I said to the clerk, a man with graying hair and beard. "I've tracked it to Brooklyn, but I don't have any other details."

The man took the printout from me and looked it over. "Interesting," he said. "Looks like those pyramids in Mexico."

"Yes," I said. "Have you seen it?"

He shook his head. "Nope, but Brooklyn's a big place." He handed the paper back. "Why do you want to find it?"

"I recently found out that someone I know painted it. I'd like to see it for myself."

The man seemed to study me for a moment. "Well, good luck."

For the next two hours, I made my way along Dekalb, meeting a number of shopkeepers, or at least their store managers, and seeing plenty of merchandise and food. But no one admitted to seeing the mural. A few commented on it, but most just shrugged off my request, busy with their day.

As the clock moved toward our lunchtime rendezvous, I worried that finding the mural would take more than a quick jaunt into Brooklyn. Parker wasn't anyone famous. He might be a skilled artist but he had no notoriety. And a thought stopped me. The mural could have been painted over, in which case, we would never find it.

My feet dragged as I neared the corner we'd decided to meet at. Neither Toby nor Candi had texted or called. That had to mean they too were coming up with zilch. Maybe we had just wasted a day.

With a smile, Toby sprang forward to greet me.

"You found it?" I said, my mood starting to lift.

"Maybe," he said.

Candi made the turn on the corner and joined us.

"Where?" I said. I was ready to head to it right then.

"Lunch first," Candi said. "I'm ravenous. Toby can tell us over hoagies. The mural's not going anywhere."

Reluctantly, I agreed and let Toby lead the way to a neighborhood deli he'd spotted on his search.

We ordered and sat at a table meant for two. With Toby's heft, we must have looked comical to the cafe's regulars, three people crowded into such a small space.

'Tell me," I blurted. "I hit a big fat zero on my blocks. I was beginning to think this was a waste of time."

Toby's smile again buoyed me. "Like I said, maybe. But I talked to a guy who said he'd seen it. 'Amazing,' he said. He gave me directions. It's kind of far."

Candi stood to pick up our order. "What's the catch?" she said. "Give me a sec to grab the sandwiches."

Then she returned. I wasn't sure I was hungry until the first bite. "What catch?" I mumbled, my mouth full of turkey hoagie.

"Candi's right," Toby said. "The guy warned me that it might be hard to get to. The business closed a few years ago."

I remembered the narrow alley in Boston behind the art gallery. "We'll find a way." I was suddenly impatient to see it. "How far?"

"Maybe twenty blocks?" Toby said, munching his roll.

"Let's drive." The quicker we could get there, the better. Every moment seemed precious.

"Yeah, driving will leave us in better shape to scale fences or otherwise trespass," Candi said.

"We're not going to break in anywhere," I countered. Unless we had to.

With lunch behind us, we drove the twenty blocks Toby directed us through to Williamsburg, and with our luck still flowing, found another parking spot.

"Now where?" I said, switching off the engine.

This block was as commercial as the previous section, but the businesses were mostly aging factory buildings.

Toby looked at the scrap of paper he'd jotted his notes on. "He said he thought it was around Thornton Street. Maybe up ahead?"

Together, we trooped along the sidewalk, eyeing each building with hope. Wherever Parker had painted the mural, it wasn't on the front of any building. A side or a rear wall was much more probable.

The next person who passed us on the sidewalk I stopped and politely asked if they'd seen the Aztec mural. The person shook their head, no. I asked another and another, assessing each person's emotions and passing up some whose vibe I didn't trust. Toby and Candi, meanwhile, continued to study the buildings.

"Here, I think," Toby called. He was several steps ahead at the next corner. I jogged up to him. Candi was already around the corner. "This fits what the first guy told me. Three stories, the cupola, the green trim."

We joined Candi. The building took up about a third of the block, and the rear was open but cut off from access by a six-foot metal fence outfitted with privacy slats. And topped with barbed wire. Still, the fencing and barbed wire were damaged in spots. It had been several years since anyone had used the premises for business or manufacturing.

"It's got to be on the rear of the building," Candi said, trying to peer through the fencing marked with *Private Property: Adams & Assoc.*

"I wish there was a way through," I said. Was the mural really here? My sun tattoo stayed quiet, providing no guidance.

Toby rattled the fence to my left, pulled a section away from the frame and motioned to me. "You're skinnier than I am. See if you can fit through here."

I looked up and down the block. No one to see me trespass. With a grunt, I scrambled through the gap, some of my hair catching in the plastic. "Let me look around," I said. "Keep an eye out."

I stood on cracked asphalt in a lot big enough to allow a freight truck to load at a docking bay and room for maybe a dozen cars. The windows on the building had been boarded up against vandals, and dried weeds from the previous fall bobbed and danced in the breeze that gusted around the space.

Candi slipped through the fence to join me. Toby stayed on the sidewalk as sentry. With his record, he didn't need to get caught trespassing.

A glimmer of red beckoned from a wall to my right, and I hurried toward it, half eager to find the mural and half anxious we would get arrested. Glancing around the abandoned space, I wondered, Who would care?

The Aztec pyramid loomed above my head, fully twenty feet across and thirty feet high, I guessed. Even in two dimensions, it commanded the viewer. Spilling over the top, the sun's rays illuminated the painted sky with deep oranges and reds. The stone stairs rising from the base were so life-like I wanted to climb them.

Candi sighed at my elbow, raising her camera to take photos. "It's totally awesome."

"It's Parker," I said, my voice catching. With quick steps, I reached the wall, at the base of the painted pyramid stairway. Just as with the scarab in Boston, I imagined my brother working here, making his careful brush strokes, his excitement building at seeing the mural take shape.

"It's too bad this is hidden away," Candi said. "What a waste."

My arm with the tattoo burned, and I reached out with that hand to touch the wall. Then I was climbing the steps. They were steeper than they looked, and the effort to move from one to the next left me panting. I lifted one foot and dragged the other one after it. Slowly, painfully. The top, with the sun just edging it, seemed the most inviting place. If I could only get there.

Come, the voice commanded, as it had in Boston.

I looked down from where I stood, not quite to the top where I would be safe. Below, on the ground, Candi screamed. Her mouth moved, but I couldn't hear her. I was enveloped in a deep silence. Toby joined Candi at the base of the pyramid.

I'm fine, I called. But my voice was caught in my throat. I turned to the sun and pulled myself up to the next step. Five more to go.

When I blinked my eyes, I was staring up at Toby and Candi. Under my back, I felt the cold hardness of the parking lot.

"Jesus, that was close," Candi said.

Toby pulled off his jacket, rolled it up and placed it under my head. "What the fuck," he said softly, concern in his eyes.

"Stop where you are," a voice commanded, but this one was real. Two police officers stood about twenty feet from us. Both had their guns drawn.

"Stay here," Candi murmured to me as I fought to get my bearings. She rose to her feet and put her hands up to show she wasn't armed. "Our friend had a seizure," she said. "But she seems to be okay now. We were looking at the mural. Her brother painted it."

The officers holstered their weapons. "Mural?" one of them said. He followed Candi's arm as it gestured to the wall. "Wow—I had no idea this was here."

The other officer approached. "Do you need us to call an ambulance for your friend?"

I pushed myself to a sitting position. "I'm fine, officer. Just blacked out for a few minutes."

He nodded. "Okay then. But we'll need to ask you all to leave this property. It's structurally unsound. Too bad about the mural. When the place crumbles, it will, too."

Supported by Toby and Candi, I walked on wobbly legs across the lot and onto the sidewalk. The officers secured the fencing, got in their patrol car and left.

The three of us moved in silence slowly along the street to our car. My head was clear once again, but I was struggling to understand what had happened on that wall.

"I'm driving," Candi said when I unlocked the doors. "Whatever's going on, you can't be blacking out at the wheel."

I knew in my gut that I would be fine driving, but I let her take the lead. I had too much to figure out.

Chapter 17

On the return trip from New York, we argued over what had happened. Candi was convinced it was a seizure. I wanted to believe the blackouts were tied to Parker. Toby suspected I had been high and risked an overdose.

"I've never had a seizure, ever." My face grew hot in anger. "It wasn't neurological."

Candi kept her eyes on the road, but glanced over at me. "And what about your mother? Maybe what she has is hereditary."

It was a possibility I had tried not to ponder. "I doubt it," I said, faking the confidence I didn't feel.

"Brain tumor," Candi said to Toby, to clue him in.

"Dr. Quinn," Toby said, "you can come clean with us. We're your friends. I've seen my share of blackouts, and yours was no different."

I heard the disappointment in his voice and felt it vibrating from him.

"Damn it," I said, turning so I could talk directly to him. "That's not it either. I have never used anything. I joke about being addicted to coffee, but beyond that—no drugs, no pills. It was Parker, or whatever he's tied up in."

By the time we dropped off Toby and headed to my condo, we had reached a truce. I would ask if my mother's tumor was a condition I was at risk for.

I made it through the weekend and the next few days without allowing myself to think so much about Parker or blackouts. I made a few phone calls attempting to unearth the history of Adams & Associates, the owners of the Brooklyn building, but got nowhere. Why Parker had chosen that business for his mural remained a mystery. Instead, I kept myself focused on work. Amanda couldn't complain about the quality of my counseling. Solid sessions, protocol followed, a full schedule of clients arranged for the next few weeks.

At my condo after work on Wednesday, I saw that my father had called twice. "I really need to speak to you," he said. "Call when you get this message."

Instead of returning the calls, I changed into shorts and sports bra and went for a run. The tension of the previous week dissipated with each stride I took.

It was after Candi arrived and we ate dinner and she told me about her day that I finally dialed my parents' number.

"It's about Mom, right?" I said when he answered.

The chemo round had not helped my mother. In fact, the cancer seemed to have thumbed its nose at the medication and had metastasized, spreading to her liver. There was little hope now that she would recover.

"Dad, I'm sorry." I tried to imagine my life without my mother in it and couldn't. It was like imagining life without air.

"I want you to convince her to enroll in a clinical trial," he said. "I've done some calling around and there's a trial up in Boston. It's an experimental drug but it looks good."

"What did Mom say?"

"She said no." My dad made a noise that might have been a sob. "I can't enroll her without her consent."

I could understand his sadness and frustration, but I also knew the power of his will as he tried, always, to bend others to his way. My mother had made a choice, and it wasn't what he wanted. Her decision gave me the strength I needed to not cave to him.

"Is she still at home?"

"Yes," he said. "They said we needed to think about hospice." This time he really was crying. It took him a moment before he could continue. I blinked away my own tears. "I don't understand her."

Because you've never tried, I wanted to say. *Just like you never tried with me or Parker.* "I'll come by Saturday once she's at the house." If anything, I would be there to back up my mother, even though I wanted her to survive as much as he said he did. I touched my sun tat out of habit. It was cool and benign. It would be a good time to tell her that Parker was very close to being found. This time for real. I hoped.

On Friday, Candi was already at the condo when I got home from work.

"Cheater Chad is finally out of my apartment," she said, folding clothes and placing them in an open suitcase. Her smile beamed. "I can move back home!"

I gave her a hug. "I've loved having you here, but hurray for you." It had been nice having another person in the condo, and a big plus that she was also my best friend. I thought of Toby and Eddi and Mrs. Carson, eating dinner around a table with a family.

"Yes, it's been a blast, but your couch was not meant to be slept on." She stuck her tongue out at me.

I threw a couch pillow at her. "I was willing to share my bed."

She threw the pillow back. "But you snore. No way."

I ordered pizza and pitched in to help her pack. In my bedroom, checking my dresser for any wayward Candi items, I spotted the astrolabe. After bringing it home from Boston, I had cleaned it up, but then had forgotten about it.

"Hey, Candi, this turned out pretty nice, huh?" I handed it to her.

She sat on the couch, moving a hand over the brass, over the stars hammered into the metal, the image of the sun and its rays bursting from one corner. "My god, Quinn. This is more beautiful than I imagined."

"I'm not a metalsmith, but the skill level seems pretty high," I agreed. "I wonder if it's worth more than I paid the guy."

Candi continued to examine the object. "If you don't want it, I'll buy it from you. I've always wanted one."

"I'll think about it," I said. "You'll have to show me how to use it. I know it's a tool for finding your location. Too bad it can't show me where to find Parker."

She stood. "You're on your own there, kiddo, but I can give you a quick lesson in terms of latitude. It's dark enough out. Let's take it outside."

I hesitated. I didn't want another surprise visit from Braden. A quick search in a kitchen drawer unearthed my pepper spray just in case. "Sure. Let's go. We've probably got another fifteen minutes until the pizza gets here."

"Before we head out into the night, I'll do some preliminaries in here." She turned the astrolabe on its side. "We're going to use it to find out the time, so first we set the date." She moved the alidade to the correct number along the scale. "Now we flip over the astrolabe to find the matching Zodiac date." She pointed to it. "Now I just need some string."

I rummaged again in my kitchen drawers until I found a small ball of twine. I couldn't remember why I had it.

Candi fastened the twine through the loop on the top of the astrolabe. "Bring a flashlight."

Fortunately, the exterior building lights were focused on the pavement, and we were able to see the sky and enough stars to make Candi happy. "We'll use Vega as our reference." She pointed out the bright star high in the eastern sky.

"Now we—" she started, but paused when a car drove into the lot, its headlights flashing across us as it turned into a parking space.

I rubbed my tattoo absent-mindedly a few times before I realized it was burning again.

"Candi," I said softly, taking her arm and guiding her into a darker area of the lot. "That car. I think it's Braden."

"We could leave for a while," she said.

"I don't think I locked the door. If we leave, it's an invitation for him to go in." I imagined my condo trashed as Braden searched for money or valuables—like I had any. "Why don't you hang out here, and I'll see what he wants."

"No way," she whispered fiercely. "We'll do this together. I don't want you to get hurt." The fear that came off her was mixed with anger, and I was touched.

"It'll be okay," I said. "Just stay a step or two behind me."

I walked briskly toward my condo, with Candi trailing. When we got to the car, sure enough, it was Braden's, with the same bumper sticker. *Adjust Your Altitude.*

I rapped on the driver's side window. "What do you want?" I put on my best don't-fuck-with-me demeanor.

He opened the door and peered up at me. "How'd you know I was here?"

I shrugged. "I figured you'd be back." From him, I sensed a cluttered mix of emotions. "You got an altitude adjustment, looks like."

"*Very* fine altitude," he said, giving me a sloppy grin.

And he drove here in that state. I cringed on the inside.

"So what's up, Braden?"

Candi inched closer. Even she could tell he was in no condition to pose a threat.

"I brought you something," he said, "but I don't want to show you out here in the dark. Can I come in?"

I weighed the chances he would recover enough to attack me or Candi. The odds were quite low, I thought, but I still gripped my pepper spray.

"For a few minutes," I said. "Then I need to help my friend with something."

He dragged himself out of the car, slipping a courier's bag across his shoulder, and followed Candi and me to my door.

Once inside, he commandeered the couch. Candi moved her suitcase, and I went to pull out paper plates for the pizza when it arrived. The more I thought about it, I couldn't throw Braden out once he'd shown me whatever he'd brought. He was too high. But I also felt uneasy at having him there.

In the living room, I perched on a chair and Candi resumed to folding her clothes.

"Do you remember stabbing Toby?" I asked.

Braden stared at me. "No. Did I?" He didn't seem particularly concerned to find this out.

"Damn it, Braden, he needed a dozen stitches. And if he hadn't been there, you would have stabbed me."

He sighed and ran a hand through his hair. "Sometimes I do stupid things."

Candi stopped folding and put her hands on her hips. "Yeah, that doesn't excuse you. Quinn went to the police."

The doorbell rang then, and Braden did a slow-motion roll from the couch. "And they're here?" He crumpled to the floor and curled himself into a ball.

"It could be," I said, savoring his discomfort. He deserved it. "But it's more likely the pizza delivery."

Five minutes later, the three of us sat around the table, eating slices of margarita. Candi was anxious—whether about Braden's presence or her anticipation of finally returning to her own place, I didn't know. Braden chewed his pizza slowly. Everything he did was in slow motion.

He seemed to have forgotten about his original mission that night—to show me whatever was in his courier bag. The few minutes we'd agreed on in the parking lot had stretched to a good half hour.

"So what did you bring with you?" I said, slipping another slice onto my plate.

"I'll get it," he said. Bringing the bag to the table, he opened the flap and slipped out a wire-bound sketchbook. The cover had splashes of color, dotted with hand-drawn stars and suns, and a detailed sketch of a man's arm including the muscles and tendons. The edges of the book looked as though they had been thumbed through often.

"Parker's?" I reached out for it, but Braden put his hands on the book, keeping mine away.

"Yes," he said. "I'll let you see it, but you can't have it. Not yet."

It belongs to *my* brother, I wanted to say, not *you*. "Fine," I said. "Just don't let anything happen to it."

"I've had it all these years and it's been safe, so don't worry." That didn't seem a great endorsement of his plans since he didn't remember stabbing Toby. Would he forget what he did with the sketchbook?

"Come on, Braden," Candi said. "Let her see it. I want to see it."

In my hands, I laid it in front of me and felt as though I had hold of a holy artifact. Carefully, I turned the pages, with Candi looking over my shoulder.

"He was really good," she said.

"*Is*," I corrected.

Images of Braden, a younger, more innocent Braden, smiling, or in a contemplative mood, or asleep. Then more images, the ones my father had seized on, of Braden in the nude. Close-ups of his arms, his legs, his torso, as Parker explored how to capture the essence of the human form.

"Thank you," I said softly. "Thank you for letting me see this."

My tattoo burned intensely, and I stopped gazing at the pages to put one hand on it. When I looked up, Parker's figure glimmered just beyond where Braden sat at the table. He had the astrolabe in his hands, and he slowly faded away.

Chapter 18

"Yeah, he was here," Braden said, watching my face. "I could feel him, too."

"What? Who?" Candi sputtered. "Where?"

"My brother," I told Candi. "He was standing over there." I pointed past Braden. Each time I saw Parker, he seemed so real yet still so ephemeral. "And he had an astrolabe. Did you see him?" I asked Braden.

"No," he said. "It's always more of a feeling, as though he's sitting or standing beside me. Sometimes he says things."

"Did he say anything this time?" I felt a twinge of jealousy, anticipating a yes.

"No," Braden said. "I just knew he was there, and then your expression … that was a giveaway."

I placed my hands on the sketchbook. "This must have brought him. Did you know it would do that?" Reluctantly, I pushed it across the table to Braden. "Keep this safe."

"Don't worry. It's my lifeline to reality." He returned the book to his bag and zipped up the top.

Candi gathered the paper plates, utensils, and glasses and carried them to the kitchen, and returned with three bottles of beer. "So where is your brother?" She opened her bottle and took a sip. "Is he dead?"

"No," Braden said, shaking his head vigorously.

"Then what the hell is he waiting for to show up in person?" she said.

I had been wrestling with that same question. "Maybe he's caught up in some kind of sci-fi time warp? An alternate universe?" I turned my beer bottle in circles, thinking. "Too out there. There has to be a more pragmatic answer."

Candi seemed to be studying the label on her own bottle. "Braden, am I wrong or do you have the same weird sense as Quinn?"

Braden slouched in his chair. His knee was not jittering, nor did I feel any dash of anxiety from him. Whatever he was on had taken him for a long ride.

"I don't want to talk about it," he said.

"Do you?" I asked. This was news to me.

"Not like you." He leaned toward me. "Parker told me you knew when you were a kid."

89

I remembered that Christmas morning long ago with the wrapped skateboard and Parker's imagined performance.

"Yes," I confirmed. "And you?"

"It's nothing like what you can do. And it's only with Parker. Was with Parker. I just…know when he's there."

"You never told me," I said. "I never knew we had this in common."

"Shut up, Quinn," he said. "Don't try to fix me."

"I'm not…I wouldn't…" Not in that way. "What's there is there. I have no more control over it than it sounds like you do."

"Exactly," he said, draining his bottle in one long swig. "I deal with it my own way."

Candi laughed without mirth. "By getting high and stabbing people. Very cool."

His head started to dip and his eyelids blinked rapidly as sleep crept up on him. "I'll admit it, I'm a mess. That's me, a royal fuck-up. Always have been."

This was familiar territory, something I heard nearly every day from my clients. "You do have a choice," I said. "And you have the strength to beat this." My words seemed lame somehow with Braden. I hit on an idea that was worth exploring. "My special ability helps me in my job, but it's been pretty much worthless in finding my brother. And I have to find him. He's in trouble. Will you help me?"

Braden had laid his head on his hands and closed his eyes, but he fluttered them open briefly. "Why not," he said. A moment later he was snoring.

Candi and I looked at each other. "I guess he's staying the night," I said. I patted him down and looked inside his courier bag, but found no knife, no other weapon.

"I'll stay one more night, so you're not alone with him," she said. She watched him sleep. "He is cute, though."

I guided her toward the living room. "He's trouble." I wished that weren't so.

Together, we finished packing the suitcase and cleaned up the kitchen. Candi would sleep with me in my bed that night, and I would lock the bedroom door just to be safe.

Despite a thorough search of the condo, neither of us could find the astrolabe.

I was awake at dawn, listening to the morning birdcall outside the window and Candi's light breath of sleep. No stirring from the rooms downstairs. Pulling on shorts and a tee, I laced on my running shoes. The meeting with my mother that day weighed on me, and once more grief swept through me like the chills of a fever. My mother was too young to die. And I was a failure as a daughter. The thing she had asked me for I had been unable to deliver.

Leaving Candi to snooze a while longer, I ventured down the stairs from the bedroom. I wasn't sure what to expect, but what I found still surprised me. Braden was gone, and nothing seemed amiss. The smell of coffee drew me to the kitchen. He had made a pot, apparently had a cup—one was in the sink—and left a note on the counter.

Thanks for the pizza. We'll find Parker.

He remembered my request, a good sign, and he had left without my having to throw him out, another good sign. But something wasn't quite right. Then I noticed the set of house keys I left hanging by the door were gone. Damn. I scolded myself. *You knew he was unpredictable.* Digging out yet another spare key—the one I kept in the coat closet on a nail, I left the condo to go for a run. A few fast miles listening to Metallica's "Enter Sandman" would leave me panting but also mellow out my thoughts. Candi could keep on sleeping.

Later that morning, after helping Candi on her way to her own place, I drove to my parents' home. The weekend stretched ahead with errands and a book I looked forward to reading. This obligation I was not looking forward to, yet I felt guilty for even thinking that. How many more times would I pull up in front of the house knowing that both of them were still alive? And when it was finally just my father living here, would I want to visit?

Gideon barked when I knocked on the door.

"You could have just let yourself in," my father said, as way of greeting. He turned from the open door and walked away from me.

I stooped to pet Gideon and followed my father.

Instead of leading me straight to their bedroom, where I assumed my mother was, he veered into the kitchen. Pouring himself a mug of coffee, he gestured to me. "Want a cup?"

Of course I did. We added our milk and sugar side by side at the counter, close but not close enough to brush shoulders. And neither of us said a word.

He sat at the kitchen table with a sigh and a frown. The mood drifting off him was somber, dark, a thickness that blanketed the room. I sat across from him and drank my coffee. It was good, at least.

"She's got to do it," he finally said.

"Is Mom still in bed?" I hadn't heard any other sounds from the house. Even Gideon was quiet, curled up near my feet, head resting on tail.

"All she does is sleep," he said. "I don't understand it. After what I've found out—she could gain a few more years, maybe more, they said. But she says no."

A few more years, but no cure. A stop gap, prolonging the inevitable. "Is she in pain?"

"I'm sure she is," he said, his frown deepening. "But she won't say. I think she's afraid that I'll force her to do this if she admits it. *Force* her?" His words were strangled.

I could feel his hurt, his grief, but I wasn't moved. The old adage about burning bridges came to mind. "Would you?"

He looked at me, his gaze fierce. "She's my *wife*. I don't want to lose her. She's your *mother*, for God's sake. Don't you care?"

He had side-stepped my question. "Can I see her now?"

He looked up at the kitchen clock and nodded. "It's time for her next dose. I'll wake her." He reached toward me, toward my hands where they encircled my mug of coffee. I shrank from him. Old habits die hard, they say. "Please," he said. "Do what you can."

My mother's face was pale against the white of the pillow, and deeply lined. Even though the weather was warm and the windows were open, she dozed under a heavy blanket. My father gently shook her shoulder, whispering in her ear words I couldn't hear. I stood at the foot of the bed. She could have been my grandmother lying there, so old she looked. And it hit me once more how fragile life was. We are handed a packet of days at our birth, but we can't take a peek to see how many we have, to know when that penultimate day arrives so we can live it to its fullest. Which day was this for Sonia Thomas?

She sat up in the bed, and my father moved several pillows behind her for support. His movements were kindly, turning back the blanket a bit, offering her a glass of water for her pill. Was this solicitousness real or a way to win her over to his side? I guessed the latter, but I had been away long enough from their day-to-day interactions that I wasn't sure.

She noticed me and smiled. "Quinn, so nice to see you." She flinched a bit as she shifted in the bed. I could feel pain and fatigue from her. That, mixed with the emotions from my father, made for a powerful brew. Gideon, who had followed us from the kitchen, sniffed once or twice and left the bedroom. Dogs can rival my ability to sense mood—they just can't discuss it with you.

"Hi, Mom." I brought a straight-backed chair that sat by the window over near the bed. "Dad, why don't you let Mom and me catch up?"

He was hovering in the room, and I didn't need him listening in, ready to critique what I'd said or not said.

"My dear, Quinn has something to discuss with you," he said as his way of having the last word. "I'll go work on getting you some breakfast."

My mother's smile was grim as he left, but she almost immediately took my hand. "I'm not doing it," she said. "He keeps asking me, but I've said no, and I'll keep saying no."

"He's frightened," I said. "And I'm sad. But it's your choice. I'll back you up, no matter what." I patted her hand.

"He's frightened because he's not getting his way for once." The force of her words left her breathless. "So be it."

"But you did think about the treatment, right?"

She searched my face. Was she looking for my opinion?

"I talked with Doctor Wallace," she said. "The oncologist. He's been straightforward about my prognosis and this experimental baloney." She paused to catch her breath. "Three months, maybe four, he said. That's all."

"That's what you'd gain?"

She nodded. "Just to prolong the suffering."

"So, you are in pain." I gripped her hand.

Her mouth set in a firm line, and she closed her eyes. "Have you found Parker?"

"I'm close," I said, forcing my optimism. "Very close. He's proving a bit secretive."

"He was always one to play it close to the vest," she said.

"Braden's seen him. So it won't be long, I'm sure." It's easy to lie when the truth hurts. I'd seen my clients do the same—*of course, I'm not using.*

I grasped for something to say. The room had gathered in the day's heat, and I could feel the dampness of my hair against the nape of my neck. Then I thought of my tattoo. If I couldn't bring a physical Parker to my mother, maybe I could conjure the holographic version. I placed my right palm over the sun and willed it to work. *Come on, Parker. Show your face.*

The minutes ticked past, with my mother now dozing. Nothing happened—no glimmer, no whisper, no nothing. I was a fool to think I could make it happen on demand.

Bending forward, I kissed my mother lightly on the forehead. "I'll stop by again soon," I whispered.

Chapter 19

My father confronted me when I headed to the front door to leave. "Did you convince her?"

I brushed past him, still bummed that Parker was a no-show. "I didn't try. She's made up her mind, and it's her decision."

He grabbed my arm to stop me. The force of his grip was still strong. "But she'll die," he said.

My anger at him softened. "Yes, she will, sooner than you or I want. But it's what she's decided, and we have to honor her wishes." I tried to remove my arm from his grasp, but he continued to hold me tight, as though keeping me near would make me listen and obey.

"I could call Robert McGuire," he said. "Get him to file the legal paperwork."

"To *force* her?" I felt a chill. "You told me you wouldn't do that."

"Because I was counting on you to make her see reason." His tone shifted into sarcasm. "But you never see things my way, so I shouldn't be surprised."

He's hurting, I told myself. *He's lashing out because he's already grieving.* But I couldn't not say what I wanted to say, what I had been wanting to say for a very long time.

"No, I don't see things your way. You made that clear when I was thirteen, when you said I was bad stuff. Parker didn't see things your way either. You gave up on both of us, long ago. I may be a disappointment to you, but I am what I am. Mom wants me to find Parker, and when I do, I'm bringing him to her." I pulled away from him.

"Your brother is dead," he said flatly, with no hint of emotion.

Taken aback, I tried to keep my face neutral. "But he's alive. Braden said —"

"That good-for-nothing scoundrel doesn't know the truth from a teapot."

"Braden has his problems. You didn't help by throwing him out along with Parker."

My father shook his head. "It's been three years."

"Three years?" His meaning became clear. "How do you know?"

"Your mother asked me to look for him, so I hired a private detective. He was able to trace his whereabouts to New York, but then the trail dried up. I filed the paperwork to declare him missing, and he's now officially declared dead."

Relief washed through me. My father had no proof—but I was also furious. "Why didn't you tell me this?"

My father continued as though I hadn't spoken. "Sonia wouldn't accept that, of course. And now you've mucked it up by putting the notion in her head that you'll find him."

"I've seen him," I said, my voice cracking, my eyes smarting from tears. "He's alive."

"Quinn, grow up. You're stuck in that mumbo-jumbo place of your childhood, hoping that people will believe your stories of ghosts and spirits."

"I'll find him," I said. "You'll see." And I walked out of the house.

My hands were shaking as I started the car and drove away. I hoped I was right.

Later that afternoon, after grocery shopping and other errands put some distance from my father's revelation, I went out onto the condo balcony to drink in some peace. The afternoon sun was behind the building, putting my little square of outdoors in a pleasant shade.

"Where are you, Parker?" I said aloud. I thought about the last several months. Finding the letters seemed to have started everything that followed. The weird sun tattoo, Braden falling back into my life, Parker's mirage, the murals and their hold on me. I wasn't sure where my mother's illness fit into it all, but I assumed there was a connection. I had to hope that Braden, despite his flaws, could really help find my brother.

My cell phone rang as I finished my mug of coffee. It was Heywood. I couldn't remember the last time he'd called me outside of work.

"Sorry to call you on a weekend," he started. His voice sounded strained. Once again I wished I could sense feelings through a phone connection.

"No problem. What's up?"

"I'm really sorry to bother you … " He drifted off into silence.

"Are you okay?" Even without sampling his emotions I knew something was very off.

"No," he said. "But it's too crazy to discuss over the phone." He paused. "And I don't want to bring this into the office."

I tried to figure out what had happened. "Are you injured?"

He laughed briefly. "I wish it were that easy."

I looked at the time. "Silver Lake, at the Nature Center? In half an hour?"

We ended the call, and I changed into clean tights and a long-sleeved Metallica tee, flinching when a horn honked in the condo lot. Whatever had rattled Heywood had put me on high alert as well.

"Hey," I said, dropping my backpack onto the park bench where he sat.

He stared off across the park meadow as though deep in thought. I sensed an undercurrent of exhaustion from him.

"You look like you could use some coffee," I said, handing him a paper cup I'd bought at the Wawa.

He took it, but made no move to drink it.

I sat beside him. "I'm listening."

He looked at his cup as though surprised to find it in his hand. "I'm not sleeping much."

"You're tired, really tired. I can see that." Heywood was divorced, no kids, but had an active off-hours life, from what he had shared. One wall of his office held team pictures of his volleyball squad, and a trophy sat on his filing cabinet. His short, dark hair and neatly trimmed goatee gave him the look of a young professor, down to the wire-rimmed glasses.

He finally looked at me, but his usual wisecracking stare was gone. This was a side of Heywood I hadn't seen. "It's the dreams. They won't stop."

"Your dreams in general or a specific dream?"

He took a drink of coffee and shook his head as if to clear it. "It's one or two. It's gotten so that I don't want to go to sleep."

Gently I chided him. "You know that troubling dreams are just a manifestation of an underlying concern."

"Yeah, yeah," he said, frowning. "I know that intellectually, but when it's my subconscious unrolling the dream, I'm there, and it's as real as my sitting here on this bench."

My colleagues and I sometimes traded therapy sessions. We were all counselors after all. But not many of them sought me out. Maybe they weren't comfortable with the truths I seemed to uncover, or maybe they felt I was too young to know what I was doing. Heywood had never shared anything deep. Our conversations, like many in an office setting, centered on movies, sports, and gossip. I wondered why he'd singled me out.

"Let's take a walk and talk," I said, slipping on my backpack. "When did the dreams start?"

Standing, with cup in hand, Heywood looked thoughtful. We walked toward the lake. "Maybe a month ago? Maybe a bit longer. It's not like I knew from the beginning they were going to repeat."

"What's troubling about them?"

Heywood made a sweeping gesture with his cup. "Everything."

"Are you comfortable describing what happens? You're not dreaming right now, so you're safe."

He slowed his steps, then inhaled slowly. "I'll try." He licked his lips and took at sip of his coffee. "There's a man, always the same man. He's in a cage or a cell, and he's reaching his arms through the bars at me, begging me to let him out. He's naked except for a tattered pair of boxers, and his skin is filthy, as if he hasn't had a bath in years. His beard is wispy, tangled. I try to reach the cage because somehow I know I can open it, but I can't move an inch closer, as if something is holding me. He screams as though he's in pain, and I can't do a damn thing about it."

The exhaustion that vibrated from him now had an added layer of anxiety as he re-experienced his dreamscape.

"That feeling of helplessness when called upon to act," I said.

"That's it exactly." He gave me a grateful look.

"You said you have a second dream?"

He sighed and ran a hand through his longish hair. "It's worse than the first."

I kept silent, waiting for him to continue. The sunlight dappled through the trees that shaded the path.

"I'm in a theater or maybe it's a planetarium, or sometimes I'm on a hilltop under a night sky. I'm alone, not another soul anywhere, maybe I'm the last person on Earth. Above me is the sun, yet it's night. It's blazing and I can look at it without going blind. But the sun is contorting itself as though it's in pain. The corona flickers and moves in jerks, and then an arm tears off and fades away. Another one goes. And the sun gets dimmer as the arms disappear. I know that when the last arm is severed, the sun will wink out and I will die."

I nodded for encouragement while trying to determine the best step forward to help him. "Powerful stuff," I said. "No wonder you can't sleep."

Heywood sipped his coffee. "I know they are just dreams, but the images are so vivid. Even now, reliving them, they are etched on my eyelids."

"You know what I'll ask next. What's been going on in your life? Something at the office? At home?"

He shrugged. "I've thought about that. And there's nothing. That's the weird thing. Aside from my sleep, I'm not particularly stressed." He crushed his cup and placed it a nearby trash container. "This really did help, though, to talk about it. To share it. Makes it less disturbing."

"Of course," I said. "Anytime you want to talk about it, I'm happy to listen."

"I think that's why I called you instead of one of the others. You're easy to talk to—no wonder your clients rave about you." He eyed me for a moment, then added, "One thing I just remembered about the dreams, especially the first one." He stopped and turned to me. "I think the guy in the cage is calling your name."

Something clicked for me then. It made sense and it didn't make sense. "Let me tell you about my brother."

I talked while we meandered closer to the lake. When I was done, he was silent, his gaze out at the water.

"Thomas, I had no idea," he finally said, looking at me. "All this time, day in and day out. How little we really know about each other, right? And here I am complaining about the shitty dreams I've been having."

"You're not getting it," I said. "Your dreams. Somehow, as weird as it sounds, they're tied to Parker. They must be."

"Bullshit," he said. "It's not possible. Before this moment, I didn't even know you had a brother."

I reached out and put a hand on his arm. "I know it doesn't make sense. But neither does this." I gestured at my sun tattoo.

"So your brother was really into the sun."

"Is," I corrected. "It's his guiding light, so to speak."

"And somehow that ink is connected to him."

"Apparently. The murals, the ink, and now your dreams. I just don't know what it all means. I'm stuck on what to do next. I think he's in trouble, but I don't know how to help him."

Heywood tucked his hands into his jean pockets. "Okay," he said at last. "Let's think through. The sun, the Ancient Egyptians, the Aztecs. What brings all of these together?"

"Something crazy," I said, remembering a lead I hadn't followed up on. "There's a name I need to look up."

"An old friend of your brother's?"

We were back at the nature center and our cars. "Not a friend. It may be a legend."

"Let me know if I can help," he said. "I owe you one." Then he smiled, the first smile since we'd met up that day. "We'll find Parker."

I had driven three blocks when I remembered that Braden's note used exactly the same words.

Chapter 20

At the office on Monday, a paper bag from the Très Bien Bakery sat on my desk. I peeked inside. Two eclairs filled with, if my nose was correct, peanut butter mousse. To die for.

"Who—" I started to say, plopping my backpack on my chair.

"You like those, right?" It was Heywood, standing in the doorway. His face was still haggard and exhaustion still poured off him, but his smile was genuine.

"I love these," I said. 'Why—"

"To say thanks. Dragging you out on a Sunday to listen to my pathetic—"

It was my turn to interrupt. "Stop. That's what friends are for."

Heywood sank into a chair and gazed at me. He looked as though he might nod off at any moment.

"But you're still not sleeping, I see." When he shook his head, I added, "Maybe try a sleeping pill? Just for a short run, to see if you can get some rest?"

I walked him to his own office and brought him a mug of coffee from the office kitchen. "Rocket fuel," I said.

At my desk, I ate one eclair, saving the other for later—much later. The day wound on, with four clients on the schedule, a staff meeting, and the endless paperwork. But always in the back of my mind, the unease over Heywood's dreams. They were his dreams, not mine, but the parallels with my own life were eerie.

I met Candi after work for a bike ride on the canal, and I filled her in on Heywood's dreams.

"Simply coincidence," she said. "Weird, yes, but coincidence." She pedaled faster, signaling that we were to sprint, and I picked up the pace. Soon I was panting, but the effort felt good. I could feel the tension easing off my shoulders as the miles sped past.

Over chocolate brownies at her apartment, I steered the conversation to the dreams. "Maybe it's Parker trying to get a message to me."

Candi rolled her eyes. "Think about this. Your colleague tells you about these dreams and casually mentions that one of the dreams included hearing your name. I don't see how that's tied to you at all. He's probably hot for you."

When I laughed, she continued. "And even if we suppose that the dreams do refer to you, why would Parker choose someone he'd never met to send you a message? That's taking an awfully big risk that your friend would mention the dreams to you, and if so, would describe them in a way that's meaningful to you, or that you would pick up on the message. A lot of ifs."

Reluctantly, I had to agree. It made no sense. But a part of me kept gnawing at it, refusing to let it go.

She must have seen the doubt on my face and patted my hand. "You of all my friends should get this. You're the counselor. You know the psychology and the physiology of it. Dreams can be troubling—hell, there are nightmares that trigger PTSD because you're reliving a traumatic event. But they aren't portals into reality. No one is communicating through dreams."

I slipped a smile on my face. "Sometimes I overthink things." I took another bite of my brownie. "There's something else, though. Not related to dreams."

I told her about the responses I'd finally received from Parker's old classmates, about the sun cult. "I have no idea where to start with that."

Candi turned to her computer. "Just a sec." She tapped a few keys and opened a page. "I took some anthropology classes a few years ago. One of the profs was an expert on ancient Egypt." She handed me a slip of paper with a name and phone number. "Tell her what you need. I'm going to guess she can help."

Buoyed by Candi's tip, I biked to my condo and even sprinted the last few blocks. When I unlocked my front door, though, the emotion that enveloped me stopped me short. The backpack on the floor next to the door was also a give away.

"Quinn," Braden said, holding a bottle of beer as he walked from the kitchen. "I wondered when you'd get home."

"You took my keys," I said. "Now you're in my house without asking."

He shrugged but smiled. "I needed a place to stay. I figured you wouldn't mind."

"What happened to your place?" Wherever that was.

"Put down your stuff and come on in." As if he owned the place. The bastard.

"You got evicted because you didn't pay your rent." When he didn't correct me, I plunged on. "What about your parents? Can't you stay with them?"

"It's easier to help you find Parker if I'm here. And you've got the couch. I don't mind sleeping there. Or," he gave me a sly look, "we could always share the bed."

"No," I said. I walked up the stairs to the bedroom to drop off my own backpack and strategize. Changing out of my biking clothes, I pulled on shorts and a tee. Having Braden as a house guest made me deeply uncomfortable, but his argument also made sense. I wouldn't have to wonder how to get in touch with him and we could pool our research. Enabler, my good sense screamed. His emotional stream was clear, though. He wasn't high.

Walking down the stairs in my bare feet, I found him sitting on the couch with the TV on.

"We can try it," I said, hands on hips. "But this is my house, and I have a few rules. In exchange for staying here, no drugs. If I see that you're using, you're out. I'll change my locks."

"No problem." He saluted me with his beer bottle. "I got a job. I'm clean. This'll work for a while."

"A job?" I shook off my doubts. *Clean?* "Where?"

"Toby helped me get it. I started yesterday."

The construction site cleanup work, I remembered. "Toby helped you after what you did to him?"

"We go back aways," Braden said. "He knows I didn't mean to hurt him."

I crossed my fingers that the job would stabilize Braden. "Well, then, hurray for you."

He wandered to the kitchen. "What have you got to eat?"

I put Braden in charge of the salad while I cooked an omelet for us. His culinary skills were better than I anticipated, but a salad is a fairly low bar to leap. The professional side of me began to worry that Braden would be more than I should take on. On the other hand, he was Parker's friend—lover, at least in the past. I could at least try to help.

Through dinner, Braden talked about the new job, and made me laugh with his astute observations about the work crew and Toby. We were loading the dishwasher when he abruptly changed the subject. "I heard you saw the murals and blacked out."

Toby. "It was nothing. I'm fine."

"Toby thought—"

"*I'm fine.*"

He closed the dishwasher and dried his hands. "I don't think so. That's another reason why I'm here."

I almost laughed out loud. "You think I need help."

"Something like that."

First Candi, then Toby, and now Braden. I was fine. They'd see.

Braden and I kept our truce over the next few days, and I found myself enjoying his company even if I did lock my bedroom door each night.

That week I also followed up on the troubling eye issue—the damn flickering at the edge of my vision—by seeing an ophthalmologist. She did a thorough exam, peered into my eyes, measured the ocular pressure, checked my acuity.

"I don't see a problem, Quinn," she said, perched on her stool. "Your vision is excellent, your retina is intact. There's no physical reason for the flickering you describe."

I was disappointed, but also relieved. "What about a brain tumor? I've blacked out a couple of times recently. Could that be the cause?"

She gave me a puzzled look. "I'm an ophthalmologist, not a neurologist. Sometimes stress can cause what appear to be vision-related issues. It's possible that could be the case with your blackouts. Have you seen your primary care provider?"

"Not yet," I admitted. "That'll be next." I had no intention of seeing him, though. Despite what my friends thought, any manifestations I was experiencing were caused by something beyond the realm of science. I just knew.

After work on Thursday, I finally took out the slip of paper that Candi had given me.

Dr. Bernice Willard. I took a breath and called.

She answered almost immediately, cautious at first, but once I identified myself as a friend of Candida Georgi, she warmed to the conversation.

I dove in. "Candi said you were an expert on the Ancient Egyptian pantheon of gods."

She chuckled. "Yes, you can put it that way. What can I help you with?"

"What do you know about Khepri?"

"Interesting," she said. "I'm usually asked about Ra. Why Khepri?"

"It's a long story, but the answer could help me find my brother."

Dr. Willard chuckled again. "Now I'm intrigued. This is more than just an idle trivia question." She paused. "Khepri was, like the superstar Ra, an Egyptian sun god. Khepri was god of the morning sun; Ra of the midday sun. A third deity, Atum, was god of the setting sun."

"That gibes with what I've read. And Khepri had the scarab face."

Braden walked in the door from work and slung his lunch bag onto the kitchen table, where I sat.

"Scarab?" he said, his eyebrows raised.

"A kind of beetle," I said, switching to speaker phone.

"Yes, with a scarab face," Dr. Willard acknowledged. "The scarab was sacred to that culture, a symbol of eternity — of birth, of death, and of rebirth. Khepri was also the god of resurrection."

I thought of Parker and his shimmering presence. Maybe he was caught in a limbo between life and death.

"He's not dead," Braden said emphatically.

Had I said that aloud?

"Who's not dead?" Dr. Willard asked. She continued gently. "You realize, of course, that these deities are not truly real. They were worshiped as any other god or greater power in other cultures but they were a human invention."

My face grew warm. "It's not that," I corrected. "I know they're myth." What had Pinscher muttered? "Do you know anything about 'the rise of Khepri'?"

I heard Dr. Willard's small gasp, and looking at Braden, he had registered it, too.

"I must say, Ms. ... " She paused.

"Quinn," I filled in. "Quinn Thomas. I'm an addiction counselor."

"Ms. Thomas." She picked up the cue. "This conversation continues to surprise me."

"Someone I know mentioned it in passing, and I believe it's connected to my brother, who's missing." When she remained silent, I added, "Some of my brother's friends said he's mixed up in a sun god cult."

"You didn't tell me that," Braden said.

Shhh, I whispered.

"I have heard of a few groups out there," Dr. Willard said, almost reluctantly. "'The rise of Khepri' refers not to the sun god's reappearance or resurrection but to his outmaneuvering Ra to gain ascendance."

"But, as you said, they're myth. Who would believe that?"

Braden laughed. "Isn't that the definition of cult? Belief in the ridiculous?"

I put a finger to my lips in a gesture to him, then spoke to the phone. "Can you put me in touch with one of the groups?"

Dr. Willard paused for a moment. "I'll try. I'd caution you to be careful. I'm sure as a psychologist you know the concept of brainwashing."

I tensed. "I'm a counselor, but yes."

She sighed. "Give me your contact information. I'll see what I can do. I don't wish to be involved, so I won't know if they choose to be in touch with you."

I repeated my name and gave her my number, then thanked her.

"What are you thinking of doing?" Braden said when I'd ended the call.

"I want to meet with them. Get them to tell me how Khepri fits into this. Then he can lead me to Parker."

"I'll go with you." Braden unpacked his lunch bag. "There's safety in numbers. And what if you black out?"

I didn't want to have to worry about Braden's state of mind while trying to get what I needed from the cultists. Still.

"In case things get weird." I nodded. "Okay."

Braden shook me awake. Three thirty in the morning. I felt a jolt of panic. The emotion was pure mine. From him, I felt only excitement. "How did you get in here?"

He knelt beside my bed. "I've got it figured out." He switched on the bedside lamp and his eager face jumped into relief. "I was searching online." I must have looked astonished, because he quickly added, "On your laptop, but I knew you'd be okay with that."

I sat up in bed. "What kind of mojo do you have? You can open a locked bedroom door without a key and login to a laptop that's not yours."

"It's the Aztecs." He waved a sheet of yellow legal pad with a rough schematic drawn on it. "The Valley of the Dead."

Aztecs? They had nothing to do with Egypt.

I yawned. "I'm ready. Let's hear it."

"Think of that New York mural. The Valley of the Dead has its own pyramids," Braden said. "And the Aztecs set them in a specific arrangement so that they had relevance to sunrises and sunsets or the moon's path across the sky."

"The Aztecs didn't build them," I said. "You're talking about Teotihuacan, a city that was old before the Aztecs showed up."

"Whatever," Braden said. "Whoever built them tracked the seasons. It was their way of telling time."

"And?" I said.

"Don't you see?" he said. "Parker's birthday is on the summer solstice. That has to be the tie to finding him."

"We wait a few weeks until his birthday, and he just shows up?" I couldn't hide the incredulity in my voice.

"Maybe," Braden said. "I think it's the answer."

Chapter 21

Sleep at that point seemed a long shot. I sent Braden down to the couch and tried to rest with my eyes wide open, staring in the dark.

If what Braden proposed was correct, I had two weeks to figure out how the summer solstice could bring Parker back—from wherever he was. I hoped the sun cult held the key, even as I shivered with worry about actually meeting them. Cults, as Dr. Willard warned, could be dangerous.

It seemed only moments later that a snake wound itself around me, an anaconda or python with glistening green scales. The sun shone overhead, but in the dappled light that streamed through the tree canopy far above. I shouted for help as the snake began to grip me tighter and tighter, but Parker's voice said, in my ear, "Stay quiet if you want to stay alive."

I turned my head to see him, but the jungle was empty. It was me and the snake and the dense vegetation. Water streamed over a nearby cataract, the rushing liquid raising a dense mist.

"What do I do?" I whispered.

The snake continued to constrict, taking my breath away. Its head was at my eye level, and it gazed at me with dark, liquid eyes, its tongue tasting the air around me.

"Wait for the right moment," Parker's voice said.

"How will I know?" I tried to scream, but the words would not form.

A shaft of sunlight cut through a gap in the leaves, shining on the snake's head.

"Now!" Parker's voice commanded.

Instinctively, I pushed against the enveloping form of the snake and it shattered, the shards of the scales falling away. I was free.

Gasping, I woke, thrashing out of the sheet wrapped around me. The morning sun lit my bedroom window. The rushing sound was the shower running in the hallway bathroom. Braden getting ready for work. He'd made it ten days.

I shook my head to clear it, and padded downstairs to start the coffee. When I glanced at my arm, another prominence had vanished.

At the office, Amanda Reed's door had a scribbled sign on it. *Meeting at ten, conference room.*

She sat at her desk, a frown on her face, but not looking at anything, not even her computer screen.

I stopped by Heywood's office before hitting mine. He still looked tired and his shoulders sagged.

"What's up?" I asked.

"Rotten dreams, no sleep, and now this." His file cabinet was open, and a stack of files sat on his desk. "We're getting a new boss. It can't get any worse."

"What?" Inwardly I cringed. "Never say it can't get worse. You'll tempt the gods."

"Ah, they're having a field day with my life already." He turned to his file stack. "I guess I should really be working on my resume, not putting any more time in on deadbeats." He sighed. "I didn't mean that."

In my own office, I surveyed my client files. I wondered what kind of changes the new director would make. How much did he care? Did I want to stay? An idea started squirming in my head. It was small and undefined and needed more thought.

At ten, the counseling team was seated around our secondhand conference table, on the mismatched chairs. Like many other things in the office, the furniture had been begged, borrowed, or possibly stolen. After all, we ran on limited funds, all of which might dry up even more.

Amanda stood at one end of the table, surveying us.

"This is a day of challenge and change," she began. "We've worked hard to help many clients get their feet back on the ground, to become productive citizens. I'm proud to have been a part of that work."

We sat silently, waiting for the news.

"I'm leaving, stepping down," she continued. There was a murmur at the table. "A new director is taking over in two weeks. He's not a counselor by training. As I understand it, he's with the Department of Education."

"What will he change?" asked a counselor named Trina. She was a single mom with two teenagers at home. Panic and anxiety filled the room but poured off her most strongly.

"I don't know," Amanda said. "I haven't met him yet." She glanced around the table. "You didn't hear it from me, but if you thought I was a tough nut about rules, Bill Morgan is as inflexible as they come—and he answers to a different set of players."

She paused to let it all sink in.

"What about you?" I asked.

She laughed. "Don't worry about me. I was thinking about a change. Now I've got to act a little sooner than I'd planned." She nodded at us. "If any of you are looking to leave as well, I'm happy to write letters of recommendation."

There were a few grumbled mutters.

"People, let's go out swinging," she said. "We are professionals."

Sitting in my office after the meeting, I felt like crying. Change is part of life, but I seemed to have won the ticket for an Extra Big Helping of Change. And I didn't like it. I didn't know which crisis to address first.

So intense was my pity party that I jumped when my phone signaled a text. A number I didn't know.

sun day meeting thursday 6:30. Come alone. You a go?

I took a breath. *Yes,* I texted. *No,* I wanted to say.

The response was immediate. An address on Olive Street in Philadelphia.

Ring bell 4x. Don't be late.

Thursday. Three days to screw up my courage.

"Penny for your thoughts?" Heywood stood in the doorway. "And it better not be, 'Where's the nearest razor blade?'"

I smiled. He was trying. "No, just weighing my next steps. Is it my brother, my mother, or my job? Flipping a coin offers only two choices, but I need three."

"If you're asking me, let's go with your brother. Then maybe I'd finally get some sleep."

"He's still the biggest unknown, though." I pointed to a chair. "Let's talk work first."

He plopped into the chair opposite me. "Do we have to?"

"What would you think if we—you and me—started our own counseling service?"

He grimaced. "Where? Out on a park bench? Take our services to the users on the street? Good one, Thomas."

I smiled. "I was thinking more of setting up *indoors* ... like at my house, or your house."

His eyebrows arched. "You're serious." It was an acknowledgment, not a question.

When I simply looked at him to confirm, he laughed. "I'm not sure I want my clients knowing where I live, or where you live either." He held up an index finger and recited, "Your safety is paramount." One of Amanda

Reed's decrees. Not everyone was delighted to attend a counseling session. Sometimes things could get dicey. Heywood was right. But…

"Our clients wouldn't be court-ordered—those would still be funneled here." I tapped my desk. "Ours would be people who know they need our help."

He shook his head. "Still, it sounds like a line I don't want to cross." When my face fell, he added, "It's not a bad idea, teaming up. A step better than going completely solo. Or working for some jerk from Education who knows nothing about counseling."

I was calculating in my head. "Rent for office space would be challenge if we're just starting out. That's why I thought my condo might work." My extra bedroom was an overflow space. I'd never added a futon or a dresser to make it into a proper a guest room. Who was going to visit anyway, I'd thought. Of course, Candi and then Braden ended up on my couch because of my decision. "I have a bedroom that could be turned into a counseling office."

We continued to discuss the possibilities now that I had volunteered my space. A business plan, a business license, finding clients, billing and administrative paperwork. Heywood wouldn't be putting anything at risk except rolling the dice that our partnership would pan out.

"It just might work," he acknowledged, a brightness in his voice that hadn't been there when he'd showed up at my office door. Relief was the emotion I pegged vibrating from him. "Aren't you even a bit worried about safety?"

"Of course." Maybe we'd hire a bouncer who could also do scheduling. "First steps first. We've got two weeks before the new boss shows up to get the process started."

After work, I paced out the spare bedroom and tried to imagine an office instead of stacked boxes of books and other odds and ends I'd never unpacked. Maybe working out of the living room would be more practical. On the first floor, I ran through several possible rearrangements in my head. *It could work.*

The home phone rang. It was my father.

"Can you come over?" No hello, no how are you, just straight to the issue, as usual.

"Not right now." I wanted to sketch out a floor plan, and do more research on what Heywood and I would need to start up a business. "Maybe tomorrow."

"Your mother's in hospice. As of today." He sounded sad and disappointed.

"It's what she wanted," I said. "I told you." Then I covered the receiver to muffle the sound of my sob. This was the final stretch, yet I had nothing for her.

"I don't know how long she has," he said. "The doctor wouldn't say—just mumbled something about a few weeks, a month…" His voice rose. "Why aren't you here? You're never here when she needs you. And she needs you now."

She doesn't need me, I thought. *He needs me — to be there, holding his hand, telling him he'll be okay even if his wife dies.* It wasn't a role I wanted.

"I'll come by tomorrow," I said. Then, to soften my response, I added, "I'm sorry, Dad. This is tough."

He was quiet so long I thought he had ended the connection. "I no longer have a son," he said at last. "And I've lost a daughter, too." Then he hung up.

Chapter 22

Braden and I sat in my car on Olive Street, where I'd managed to find a parking spot. It was six twenty, and the three-story rowhouse that was the destination was three doors up.

"You can't come in with me," I said for what must have been the fiftieth time that day.

"You're not going in by yourself." His repeated response.

I had learned over the last several weeks the steeliness that lay at Braden's core—when he wasn't high. But he was still a loose cannon, and because of that, I was panicked. This could go very wrong.

"In five minutes, I'm walking up the street and ringing the bell," I said. "They'll nix the whole thing if you're with me. We will have made the trip for nothing. And Parker will still be missing."

"They'll let both of us in." His lips closed into a firm line.

"You do see the irony of your argument? You want to act as my bodyguard—you who broke into my condo and held a knife to my neck."

He waved a hand. "That was then. This is now."

I shook my head and sighed. "Okay, let's go."

Out on the street, the early evening was quiet. A few people strolled ahead of us, and at the far end of the block, several kids rode skateboards. It was a pleasant neighborhood, not one I pictured as home to a cult.

My watch said one minute before six thirty. I stood on the step of the rowhouse and pressed the doorbell four times in quick succession. Braden placed himself to one side, perhaps hoping to stay out of view of the peephole in the door.

Within a moment, several locks turned and the door opened. A middle-aged man with a neatly trimmed beard peered out at me, then at Braden.

"You were to come alone." His words were disapproving, but I sensed his curiosity.

Braden stepped forward. "It's my fault. She planned to, but I wouldn't let her. So you let both of us in."

"Fortes fortuna iuvat," the man said, opening the door wider. "Fortune favors the brave. I'm Khufu." He turned away and we followed him into the house.

Brave? I wondered where bravery ended and foolishness began.

I expected black walls painted with satanic symbols that glowed in an eerie light. Instead, we stepped into a modest living space, newer but comfortable couch, a full bookcase, a Persian rug. Normal stuff. And empty of people.

"I thought we were meeting a group?" I said.

"We're all on the roof," Khufu explained. "That's where we meet. Getting there's a bit tricky, but it's safe."

I walked behind him up two flights of stairs, Braden at my heels. Watching Khufu's broad shoulders and back as he climbed the steps, a sense of dread filled me. He was strong. And the scarab tattooed on his neck portended that the evening wouldn't be normal.

On the third floor, Khufu escorted us to a slim ladder that ascended into the ceiling.

"Just up there. Someone will help you onto the roof."

I took a breath, grasped the rungs and climbed cautiously. Above me, a patch of blue—a clear evening—beckoned. As my head emerged into the open air, hands took hold of my arms and shoulders and helped pull me up. I turned to help Braden but he was already out. With little effort, Khufu stepped out into the roof's flat expanse. Surrounding us were other roofs of rowhomes and to the south by a dozen blocks, the high-rise buildings of Center City. The sun was still well above the horizon.

The center of the black roof was painted with a golden sun, maybe twenty feet across. Deck chairs were set in a semi circle atop the sun, but no one was sitting. Six men eyed us, and at least four had visible scarab tattoos like Khufu. Two wore long, dark robes. The others were dressed as Khufu, in jeans and tees. They all seemed to be in their thirties and forties.

One stepped forward to shake my hand. "Welcome. I'm Hatshepsut." He gestured at the others. "That's Thutmose, Ramses, Amenhotep—"

"You're all named after the Pharaohs?" I interrupted.

Khufu laughed. "What we call ourselves outside of this realm is much different." Then he frowned. "We invited you in tonight because my contact said you had pressing business with Khepri. Whatever you learn, hear, or see here stays within this sacred space. You must agree or I will escort you out."

Seven somber faces waited for my answer. *These guys are serious.* I had told myself that before coming there, but their expression confirmed it.

"Of course," I said. Braden nodded his assent.

"Then we begin," Khufu said.

A chiminea sat in the middle of the semicircle of chairs alongside a stack of wood. One of the group started a fire with kindling and added chunks of wood as it caught. The others fanned their chairs around it—not too near since the evening was still warm. Braden and I took the two chairs offered us. Absently, I rubbed my tattoo through my sleeve. It had started a slow burn when I stepped onto the roof.

Khufu stood beside his chair and raised his arms as though commanding the heavens. He recited:

O sun!
Burn the great sphere thou mov'st in; darkling stand
The varying shore o' the world.

The others murmured their response in unison, "Khepri, who sees and hears all things."

A bloom of smoke immediately rose from the chiminea, and a shiver ran up my spine. I felt no animosity from the group, but the unbridled joy that erupted with the appearance of the smoke unnerved me.

"We are here this evening to honor you, Khepri, whose ascendance we believe in." Khufu kept his arms outstretched in supplication. "We have two guests with us, and one is in need of your help." Another bloom of smoke rose, and he turned to me. "Khepri will listen. Stand and address him."

Things were moving faster than I'd planned. I had dozens of questions to ask—and none of them were about talking to a mythological being. But I stood and gathered my thoughts.

"My brother, Parker, has been missing for several years. Somehow Khepri is connected with that. The sun was my brother's symbol, and as an artist, he often incorporated the sun's image in his work. Can any of you help me find him?"

I paused and when group remained silent, I sank into my chair. What else did they want?

Braden stood up. "I'll add that Parker's an old, old friend, someone I would have given my life for." He paused. "And I still would, to bring him back."

No, I thought. It should be me giving up my life to save him, not Braden.

The smoke rose lazily from the fire, and the group stayed silent, their heads bowed as though in prayer.

Then Khufu raised his arms again and intoned words that I guessed were Egyptian.

I puzzled over the mishmash of their liturgy. Greek, Latin, Shakespearean, Egyptian. They're making it up as they go. Which meant they were totally unpredictable.

The fire tender added more wood to the chiminea, causing flames to flicker out from the top.

"Thutmose will tell us what Khepri decides," Khufu said.

A man in a dark blue flowing robe had his eyes closed, his palms facing upward. The rest of the group turned their attention to him.

"This is bullshit," Braden whispered.

I frowned at him, finger to my lips. We were at least three stories above the ground, with no railing around the roof's perimeter. I did not want to be tossed over the edge because we disrespected the group's deity.

Thutmose moaned and tossed his head. "Not yet, not yet," he said softly. "When the sun edges the horizon, he will answer."

Khufu nodded. "And so we wait. And while we wait, we eat." He pulled back a covering draped over a folding table at one corner of the roof. Dishes of hummus, flatbreads, kibbe, tabbouleh. The aroma of the foods mingled with the smoke. "It's potluck," he said to me. "Help yourself."

"Let's see if they eat the food," Braden murmured. "You never know…"

"Oh, come on," I said. "Why would they—" I stopped. Anything was possible.

Once the group filled their plates, Braden and I followed. The group talked softly with one another as the sun sank, illuminating with a deep orange the clouds in the west. The food was good and there was plenty of it.

"Thank you for sharing this with us," I said to Khufu when I went back for another kibbe.

He smiled, the first time since we'd arrived. "You're welcome. We hope that you might consider joining us as a member. You have a strong inner power. Khepri appreciates that."

Astonished, I could only stutter, "Thanks." Dr. Willard's words came back to me. Be careful.

Back at my seat, I threw out a question that had been nagging me since I'd arrived. "Why do you worship Khepri in the evening if he's the god of the rising sun?"

Ramses answered, waving a piece of flatbread. "Because he is truly god of all the day. We favor him over Ra or Atum."

Khufu added more quietly, "We aren't early risers, none of us. We like evenings better."

Several in group laughed.

Dinner finished, but daylight still left, the group passed around a joint. I politely declined, but Braden accepted it, drawing deeply. *Great move for a bodyguard.* When he saw my look, he just shrugged.

As the joint made its rounds, I threw out another question. "Do any of you know the artist Pinscher?" I had finally placed Khufu's cryptic greeting. Pinscher had used that same Latin phrase the day I was in his shop.

"Of course," Khufu said. "We owe our scarabs to him. And you? Did he ink your arm?"

Involuntarily, I looked down, but my sleeve covered the sun tat. I had not shown it to anyone there. "No," I said, once again unnerved. "My brother drew it."

"And now he's missing," he said. "He must have displeased Khepri. We must fix that."

At that point, the fire tender added a handful of dried herbs to the fire, which created a fragrant smoke that wafted across the roof. I breathed in the heady scent and relaxed slightly.

Khufu stood again. "Thutmose is ready to relay the response."

My eyes blinked and I felt myself lighten, almost lift from my chair. I gripped the chair sides to keep me stable.

Thutmose, who had the hood of his robe up, moaned again and then stared straight at me. "The sun flings off its radiance to draw you in, but you resist. The more you push back, the farther away is your destiny."

Through the sweet smoke, Parker's image shimmered. His face was streaked with mud and his arms were outstretched toward me.

It's not safe, he whispered.

"What isn't safe?" I breathed, reaching for Braden's arm to let him know. But Braden was passed out in his chair. The rest of the group swayed in slow motion, chanting, low and measured, "Khe-pri, Khe-pri, Khe-pri."

The fire tender tossed on another bundle of herbs, and the smoke billowed out, obscuring Thutmose and the rest of the group. Parker vanished into the haze, and a sob escaped me. To my right, out on the roof's edge, a small figure of a man—he couldn't have been more than two feet high—gestured at me. Come, he seemed to be saying. Then the figure dissolved, just as Parker had, and was gone.

Someone's hands found my arm, and Thutmose knelt before me. He pulled up my sleeve, revealing the sun tattoo, and ran a finger over it. But unlike Pinscher's touch, Thutmose's was rough and hot. He folded back his hood and turned his gaze to me.

"Let yourself go," he growled. "It is time."

We are seated cross-legged in a circle, knees touching knees. A tight circle on ground that shifts slightly with each exhalation of breath. The air is clear and clean, and the sun shines from high in the sky.

I don't need to look around the circle. I know all of them even though we have only just met. I can touch their inner selves, know their secrets, and they are dark secrets. They have done things better left unsaid.

In the center of the circle, a flame burns, emanating from a point I can't quite focus on. Each time I try, the flame and its source readjust.

Breathe in, breathe out, the voices say. They echo and ring in the clear, clean air. And as one, we breathe in and we breathe out, a sad sighing that makes the sun go dim.

From the sky fall dark blue beetles the size of my fist. They drop into the circle and crawl to us and over us. Their mandibles bite into our skin and we bleed, and the beetles drink the blood and become bluer, a blue so pure and so real that I weep at the beauty.

The sun descends into the circle and one of the beetles crawls onto its face, grasping the edge of the solar disc with its six perfect legs. The sun arches up into the heavens, carrying the beetle with it.

With the sun at its apex, the ground shifts violently, throwing those of us in the circle against each other. As I gaze up at the sun, the beetle clutches the solar disc, making the sun contract and contort as though in pain. And I am in pain, unbearable pain, and I scream. But no one hears me.

I opened my eyes to a sky that was inky beyond the gleam of the city lights. I was once again on the rooftop. The cult members were still there, but in their chairs and as inert as I felt. Each movement I tried was weighted and sluggish. The smoke from the herbs had been overpowering.

"Quinn," Braden whispered. He was shaking me awake. "You shouted. We've got to leave—now. While they're still out cold."

"What happened? I don't remember—"

"Quiet," he hissed.

The panic from him mixed with the panic rising in me. "My hand, my arm. It's tied to the chair…" *What the fuck?*

"Jesus," he said. He fumbled with the cord, cursing under his breath. "Who did this? The knot's tight. I can't loosen it."

"The table," I said softly. "There was a knife on it."

Braden's form moved across the roof, quickly but carefully around the slumbering men. He sawed through the dense cord for several moments until it parted and my arm was free.

We felt our way to the ladder and heard a stirring within the group.

"Hurry," Braden said. "You first. I'll bring up the rear in case they try anything."

My legs felt like lead, each step dragging against gravity. We made it down the ladder and through the house to the front door. I thought I could hear faint voices behind us. He turned the locks and we stepped onto the street, shutting the door behind us.

Stumbling along the street, we got into my car. I sped past the rowhouse as the front door burst open and Khufu stood, backlit by the light within.

Chapter 23

I woke from a dreamless sleep and rolled over in bed. The hours on the row-house roof came crashing down on me and I sat up fully awake. I had a dim memory of the drive home, riding in silence with Braden as the miles slipped past. Somehow I had ended up in my bed, still fully clothed. Had I blacked out again?

Running a hand through my hair, I made a futile attempt to tame it and splashed water on my face to help erase the last vestiges of sleep.

At the bottom of the stairs, I stood listening for a moment. All was quiet. No emotional wave from anyone but myself.

"Braden?" I called.

The couch was empty, the coffee pot clean and unused yet for the day, no sign of Braden anywhere. And no note.

I tried to remember if he'd returned with me. We'd been in the car, but beyond that, I couldn't bring back any recollection of our arrival at the condo.

He had done the vital thing, though. He had rescued me on that roof.

I tried calling his phone, but it went to voicemail. Giving up, I made a pot of coffee, then showered and got ready for work. I still felt sluggish, and even after a mug of java, my mind had trouble focusing. When I reached for my backpack, I caught a flicker of movement and stopped. Crawling across the pack was a blue dung beetle, a scarab. The broom made quick work of it, and I swept the dead insect out the front door and off the steps.

Spooked, I looked out at the parking lot but saw nothing amiss.

In the car, I locked my doors, and then jumped when my cell phone rang. It was Toby, and I relaxed slightly.

"I'm just heading into the office," I said. "Is all okay?"

"Maybe," he said. "I should be heading off to work myself, but Braden showed up. Banged on the door, scared my mom—and she doesn't scare easy."

"How is he? We were out last night…it's a long story…" I wasn't sure Toby would believe me if I told him.

"He was baked on his ass and wanted a place to crash. I thought he was staying with you. He knows we've got a big job this week."

My mind started to spin. "He's using again? He's been clean for weeks."

"He wouldn't talk about it. He was closed up. What happened?"

"He saved my life." *Damn it.* This couldn't be happening. "I thought he would hang in there. You made it, I was sure he could, too."

Toby was quiet for a beat. "Quinn…"

I sucked in my breath. The day was not getting any better. "Things have…changed?"

"It's not what you think."

No, I wanted to shout. He wasn't the first to stray and he wouldn't be the last, but I cried on the inside. Braden, then Toby—the two men I realized in that moment I truly cared for. Hell, maybe even loved. "Sure," I said, neutral now.

"It was only this once."

Sobriety is a journey, I reminded myself. I felt like screaming, *You idiot! You had it nailed!*

Instead, I offered only professional feedback. "What are your plans? Once is still using, you know." Once would lead to twice, and then three times, and before you knew it, you were in the shit big time.

He sighed. "I have some things to figure out."

"If you want help with that, I'm here. Or go see Heywood. He's good, maybe even better than me."

I could almost hear him shake his head. "Mostly, it's you," he said.

"Me?"

"I think I love you." Then he hung up.

In my office, I laid my head on my desk and closed my eyes. I had been there only five minutes.

"Thomas," Heywood called from the doorway.

I heard his footsteps on the carpet, crossing to my side. "I'm not going to make it today," I said, and raised my head. "I need a favor."

"We're not even business partners yet and you want a favor?' But his eyes twinkled.

"It's a long story that I'll tell you at another time. Tell Amanda I'm taking a personal day. I wouldn't do my clients any good if I stayed."

Heywood pretended to take out a notebook. "I'm marking that down. You owe me one. Now get out of here."

My car's a/c decided to take the day off, too, so I drove to my parents' house with the windows open and the fan fins aimed at my face. Sweat dampened my scalp and left me sticking to my faux leather driver's seat.

Gideon bounded out of the house to greet me when my father opened the front door.

"Finally," he said, but he also took a moment to look out onto the porch, checking, I guessed, if I'd brought my long-lost brother with me.

I scooped up Gideon and brought him with me into the house. The mood that vibrated through the living room—the entire house from what I could tell—was sadness, deep and dense. Nothing new from the last time except maybe thicker.

My father motioned me to the kitchen. His eyes were red-rimmed, but he was as crisp and curt as usual. He was not a hugging man.

I set Gideon down, and checked the coffee pot. Still at least a cup left. I filled a mug and heated it in the microwave, still waiting for my father to say something. When I finally seated myself across from him at the kitchen table, he nodded once.

"She's asleep," he said. "The hospice nurse is due around five for her evening round of medication."

"How lucid is she?" I stirred sugar into my mug, watching the liquid swirl so I wouldn't have to look at my father.

"She knows I'm there when I go in."

"I'd like to stay until she wakes, spend some time with her."

"What about your work?" He put the emphasis on "work," giving it a downward spin, his meaning clear.

"Let me worry about that."

"Back in my day, druggies were best left on the street corners where they belong, not pampered."

I dug my fingernails into the palm of my hand to keep from reacting. "It's a disease, Dad. They need help." I decided the best tack was to change the subject. "What about the funeral? What does Mom want?"

My father's mood abruptly turned to anger and his eyes narrowed. "She's not dead."

"But she's in hospice." I tempered my tone. "Do you want me to make some calls? Find out what your options are?"

"No!" he said fiercely. As though his not making plans for the inevitable would delay her death.

"I'll keep my offer on the table if you change your mind," I said, then stood and put my coffee mug in the sink. "I'm going to sit with her awhile, even if she's sleeping."

He put out a hand to stop me. "You're right," he said with a sigh, but not making eye contact. "I just can't face any details like that right now."

My mother looked at peace as she slept. Once again, I pulled the chair over from the window to sit beside her. The blinds were turned to keep out the bright sun of the afternoon, but not so much that it made the room gloomy. The oak dresser, the cream walls, the deep purple of the window treatment were all her doing, her eye for interior design—something I didn't inherit.

She had offered suggestions for my condo, but with my limited budget, the most I had done was buy a deeply discounted couch in beige, the color she recommended. I'd relied on Candi for the rest of my furniture, which thanks to my friend's creative super sense somehow matched despite their varied histories and low price tags.

It was the print above the bed that caught my eye that day, though. A stark landscape at dusk, with bare branches thrust up from the trees that flanked the artist's view. The sky darkening, a setting sun still vibrant but a harbinger of the night ahead. How long had this print been here? It had a familiarity about it, but I didn't remember it.

I leaned forward and kissed her forehead, then settled in the chair. She had been the first one to caution me about my special sense. The first time, when my kindergarten teacher sent home a note. *Quinn sees things that aren't there.*

You're special, my mother had said. *You have a gift that most people don't have, and they won't like you for that.*

"Like Parker can draw?" I responded.

She nodded. "Yes, but drawing is something that people can relate to and enjoy. Your gift is rarer and scarier for people." *Including your father,* she later said.

She had been right, on both counts, and her counsel had kept me safe more often than I could tally. No one wants to think that you can read their mind—even though I can't.

Pushing those thoughts aside, I let my grief surge to the surface. What would I do without her?

Wrapped in sadness and dragged down by exhaustion from the night before, I finally dozed, and woke to my arm on fire. My mother was also awake, looking at me through half-open lids. Rubbing my arm, I looked at the tattoo and flinched when I saw that another prominence had vanished. I felt again the coarse touch of Thutmose, his leering gaze, my arm held fast to the chair.

I reached out for my mother's hand and squeezed it. "You're awake."

"Sleep, wake, sleep, wake. It's all I do anymore," she said, squeezing back. It was such a slight squeeze I almost missed it.

"The nurse has been coming by twice a day, Dad said."

The corners of my mother's mouth turned up a bit. "She's nice." Her voice was a whisper but still clear. "Not much longer, I think."

My eyes smarted. I didn't want to cry in front of her, so I looked up to clear my vision, blinking rapidly. "The painting above the bed. Is it new?"

She peered up at it. "Oh," she said, and when she looked at me, there was a hint of mischief. "I asked your father to get it framed. I like it."

I had trouble following her words, though, because the tattoo was a burning distraction. Without thinking, I took my mother's hand and placed it on the sun. Maybe I thought her touch would be a salve.

The burning stopped immediately, but she gasped at the touch, then sighed in relief. "Oh my god," she said. "You're here."

She wasn't looking at me, but at the foot of the bed. In that space, Parker stood, shimmering in his other-worldly vision that I'd just seen not twenty-four hours before. He wasn't reaching out to me this time, but his thin face and ragged beard made me hesitate before speaking.

"She's dying, Parker," I finally said. "Cancer. She's in hospice."

I know, his voice whispered in my head. *You made the bridge. Thank you.*

"I'm so sorry," my mother said softly. "Look how you're suffering. You didn't deserve any of it."

They gazed at each other for several moments.

Tell her ... tell her I forgive her.

I passed on his words, not sure why I could hear him when she couldn't.

"And I'm sorry, Mom," I told her. "I'm sorry I can't get him here in person."

She made a weak wave of dismissal with her other hand. "He's here. I'm not dreaming this."

Tell her thanks for that. He gestured to the framed print above the bed.

Her smile widened when I relayed the message. "I kept it rolled up in the closet for so many years. Your father never found it."

I looked from my mother to Parker and back. "It's Parker's?" No wonder it had a familiarity about it.

I finished it just before — I wanted her to have something of me, his voice whispered in my head.

I realized then why my mother had kept Parker's letters to me hidden away. Why they looked like they had been unfolded and refolded so many times. They were more pieces of him she could hold onto when he was no longer anywhere near.

"It's now where it belongs," my mother murmured. "On display." She turned to me. "Promise me you'll take it when I'm gone."

"Of course," I said. The sun was setting in the picture, never to dip below the horizon. But too soon, my mother would do so.

The sun reminded me of the rooftop nightmare and the morning's news. "Braden's struggling," I said to Parker.

He's stronger than you think, he whispered. *I'm the one who fucked up. I just didn't know.*

"Tell me where you are, and I'll rescue you."

I don't think you can.

"Sonia," my father shouted from the doorway of the bedroom. "What the hell is going on in here?"

Startled, I pulled my arm from my mother's touch. Parker's image flickered out, and my mother put her hand to her mouth with a soft moan. *No, I thought, I need to know how to find you before it's too late.*

My father strode to the bedside. "What nonsense are you telling her?" He scanned the room, as though looking for the secret we had been sharing.

"He's alive, Alan," she said, wonder in her voice. "I knew he was."

The look he gave me made me shrink against the chair. Anger boiled off him, more virulent than what I'd sensed in the kitchen. He grabbed my arm and pulled me off the chair, away from the bed.

"You little bitch," he said in my ear, so only I could hear.

"Alan, stop," my mother said, struggling to sit up.

I yanked my arm free. "It's fine, Mom." Coolly, daring my father to stop me, I moved to her side and kissed her cheek. "I'm going now."

She patted my own cheek. "Thank you," she breathed, a tear spilling out as she blinked.

"Quinn," my father barked. "Now."

Giving my mother a quick smile, I marched past my father. "I'll let myself out."

Gideon, who had been waiting outside the bedroom, trotted at my heels. I shouldered my backpack, took a last look around the living room, and walked out the door.

I pondered briefly if that was the last time I'd see her alive.

Chapter 24

Mentally and physically drained, I collapsed on my bed and tried to nap. I'd begged the day off, I might as well pamper myself. To my surprise, I slept solidly for three hours and woke to the buzz of a text message.

we have unfinished biz

Khufu, or whatever his name was outside his rooftop lair. I deleted the text and tried Braden's phone again. Again, I got no answer — and his mailbox was full. A lot of good he would do me strung out. But I missed him. And I shivered at a sudden thought. What if the sun cult had found him?

I paced around the condo, my worry building to a crescendo. Finally, with several hours still left of daylight, I changed into biking gear and pedaled to the canal. I kicked my workout into a real burn, cranking up Black Sabbath's "Changes." But behind each tree along the path, I imagined a cult member waiting for me.

When I came out of my trance, I had ridden eight miles farther than my usual turnaround,. My legs ached and I was bone-tired, but it didn't matter. The canal was quiet at that hour, no walkers or other bikers to share the towpath with, which suddenly seemed especially eerie. I wiped my eyes, drying the tears that kept welling up when I thought of my mother — and Braden and the rest of my sorry life.

Trust in yourself, Pinscher had said. At the time, his words seemed to hold such power, but now I saw them as a phrase empty of any real value. I had trusted in myself, and it had gotten me and those around me in trouble.

I took a deep draft from my water bottle, turned my bike around and headed south, to home. The faster I pedaled, the fewer crazy thoughts bounced around in my head. With the music switched off, all I heard was the rush of the wind through my helmet, and the crunch of the gravel under my tires. Everything else was drowned out.

The buzzing in my pocket finally got through to me. I pulled up, and took out my phone, surprised that I had reception along that stretch of the towpath.

It was Candi — not Khufu, as I'd feared. "Where have you been?" She sounded annoyed. "I've been trying to reach you for the last hour."

"Putting in some miles." I wiped my face with a bandanna. My entire body felt damp with sweat.

"Without me?" But she didn't sound too put out.

"I needed to clear my head—too many thoughts racing in a hamster wheel."

She laughed. "Speaking of racing, only two weeks left. I've got to get my butt back on the bike." Our annual ride through Chester County farm country. Fifty miles through undulating hills. Other entrants cared about time. Candi and I did it for the right to eat double-decker waffle cones at the finish line.

"I'll be back at the condo in about twenty-five minutes. I can call you then. I've got lots to catch you up on."

"The Brandywine Notch," she said.

I had no idea what she meant. "A notorious hang-out for a band of thieves?"

"Much, much better," she said. "Think solstice. I'll be by your place in a bit. Don't start dinner. I'm bringing it."

That was enough motivation to power me through the remaining distance home. Legs burning from the effort, I stowed my bike, showered, and had the table set by the time Candi showed up with take-out from our favorite sushi restaurant.

"You look totally beat," she said, as she unpacked the plastic bag. "You are so going to smoke me in the race."

I opened the containers, breathed in the aromas of rice and pickled ginger, and went to the kitchen to hunt up chopsticks. "It was more than just the mileage." I told her about the cult and Braden and my mother in hospice—and Parker's appearance twice in two days.

"Oh my god, girl, no wonder you're freaking." She waved a chopstick. "A rooftop cult. And I led you to it."

Returning to the kitchen, I brought back two beers. "It's not your fault. I was one who pushed Dr. Willard to meet them. She warned me." I pushed Khufu's image out of my mind. "What's this about a notch?"

Candi moved several more rolls onto her plate. "I was doing more research for a patron and ran across a mention of it. Pretty obscure—no website—but I found a newspaper article from several years ago. It's sort of the same idea as Stonehenge, but on a minuscule scale."

Each year, on the morning of the summer solstice, she said, the sun's rays spilled through a narrow crevice in a granite formation along the Brandywine Creek. It happened only on that day, no other.

"The article speculated that the Lenape identified the Notch and used it in a ceremonial rite," she said. "The other theory was that it was noticed more recently, like, say, in the mid-1960s, by a few stoned hippies camping out."

I dipped a sweet potato roll in wasabi. "Interesting, but so what?"

"I think it's the connection we've been looking for." She looked thoughtful. "Didn't you say Braden's theory pointed to the Aztecs? Based on the New York pyramid?"

Whoever built them tracked the seasons. I saw his face, full of excitement, and I sighed. "I still don't get it."

"Speaking of Braden, have you heard from him?"

I stacked our plates and trays and kept my gaze down so she couldn't see my reaction. "I don't know if I will. But I owe him. He's got to know that."

"What's going on with Toby?" She cleared the rest of the table and wiped it clean.

I stopped loading the dishwasher and leaned on the counter, facing her. "He told me he loved me." When her jaw dropped, I added, "That was after he admitted he'd backslid."

"And do you have feelings for him?"

"No," I said. "Yes." When she chuckled, I added, "It's complicated. Maybe it's a good thing I've been his counselor. I'm not allowed to cross that line."

"You need to find another Jude." She scrounged in my cabinets for dessert and found a package of Oreos.

"Yeah, except that didn't work out, remember?" Then because I didn't want to think about Jude or Toby or Braden, I switched the subject. "Let's talk about the Notch. I'm still not following your train of thought on it."

She sat on one of the couch and I on the other, her tossing Oreos at me. They were stale, but still edible.

"Point number one, the sun god Khepri is somehow involved. Creepy, but seems to be true. Point two, the summer solstice is nearly here and its focus is the sun. Point three, you've got a weird sun tattoo that's tied to your brother." She bit into a cookie, and spoke with a mouthful. "Point four—"

Finally catching her drift, I cut in. "Parker's birthday is the summer solstice. And point five, you're guessing that if I show up at the Notch at the appointed time, Parker will somehow appear."

She raised a fist in confirmation and took another cookie from the bag.

"That's exactly what Braden said." I blew out a breath. "Okay, what the hell."

We sketched out a plan. The race would happen on a Saturday, the day before the actual solstice, and we would return early on solstice day to climb to the Notch.

"I need to find out exactly where it is," Candi admitted. "It might be on private property."

"I thought you said people gathered there. It must be a public space."

She frowned. "Or the sun worshipers go there anyway."

Sun worshipers…the cult…My enthusiasm dropped markedly. "What if Khufu and his gang show up?"

"They won't," she said.

I said nothing.

"We'll bring our own army. They won't touch you. Don't worry."

Our talk turned to work, and I floated my plan to partner with Heywood. Somehow it didn't seem as strong an idea as when I'd pitched it to Jeremiah, but Candi lit up, a smile on her face.

"Perfect!" she said. Sliding off the couch, she hurried upstairs to my extra bedroom, and I followed behind. The room held my bike, several boxes of books, a stuffed chair a friend had passed on to me but that I didn't like, my cross-country skis, and a few other boxes the contents of which I couldn't recall. She turned in a circle, taking it all in. "It will work."

This was Candi's forte. Without her help, the rest of my condo would consist of rickety chairs, chipped and cracked bookshelves, and bare walls. Somehow she had found affordable pieces that looked like they were made for one another. It was a space I thrived in because it brought me pleasure.

"Give me a week, maybe a smidge more, and I'll have you fitted out with an office in here." She pointed at the boxes. "Gotta get rid of these. That's your assignment. I'll take care of the rest."

The reality of the challenges ahead felt almost as frightening as facing the cult. Could I make a go of this solo work? Almost solo—Heywood and I would have each other's back. I hoped.

Closing the door to the spare room, Candi headed to the living room. "Are you worried about safety?"

"Heywood's also worried about that," I said. "We'll screen our clients, and we can run interference for each other."

"You might think about someone to answer the phone, schedule appointments, make coffee." She took one last Oreo and carried the bag to the kitchen. "I'll ask around, see if anyone is looking for some part-time work."

I saw my bank account dwindling, paying an employee, paying a bookkeeper, paying business fees, hoping for clients. Maybe I should be dusting off my resume, too, instead of digging myself—and Heywood—into debt.

"I'll think about it," I finally said.

My phone buzzed, and I dug it out of my backpack. It was Toby. Candi looked over my shoulder to read the text.

I need to see you.

It was going on nine in the evening. I had to work in the morning. Candi elbowed me, gently. "You're going to have to set him straight," she said, grinning. "I'm out of here."

Tonight? I texted. I realized I really wanted to see him, too.

His text returned immediately. *Yes.*

Sure. Come on over.

"Hey," Candi said, from the doorway. "Quinn Thomas is a popular gal this evening."

Just beyond her, on the front step, stood a familiar figure.

"It's fine, Candi. Let him in. It's Pinscher."

The look she gave me said, *Are you cool with this guy?* "Of course," I said, and she was gone. Pinscher stepped inside and closed the door.

"What are you doing here?" I blurted, but then quickly backpedaled. "Sorry. I'm just surprised to see you. Want a beer?"

He nodded and followed me into the living room.

"Take a seat. I'll be right back." I opened two bottles while trying to calm myself. How had he found me? And why?

I handed him the beer, took a sip from my own, and settled once again on the lone stuffed chair. This must be kismet to eternally return to this chair.

"It wasn't hard to find you," Pinscher said, looking at the label and presumably finding the ale satisfactory. He turned his gaze to me. "You must be wondering what brought me here."

Just as at the dark arts shop, I felt reality shift for a moment. The room flickered and then readjusted to some frequency that seemed compatible with my guest. I still didn't know who or what he was, but I knew why he was there.

"My tattoo," I said.

Chapter 25

"Yes, it's the tattoo," Pinscher said. "But it's more than that. If you remember, I've said you are a conduit. The tattoo is the catalyst, but without you, it would be nothing more than a slip of paper. A fine rendering of a glorious sun, yes, but more or less just a drawing."

Pulling my feet into a cross-legged position on the chair, I waited a beat, but he said nothing else. "There has to be something else to bring you all this way, and at night."

He smiled slightly. "The night hours can be the best on the clock."

I thought of Braden, a night owl haunting my condo. First, as an intruder and then as a collaborator. And now where was he?

Pinscher leaned forward, elbows resting on his knees, the crab on his right hand eyeing me. "Your emotional radar may have gone unnoticed for much of your young life, but the tattoo causes you to shine like a beacon. That beacon is stronger now than it was the last time we met, and that time was stronger than the first time you brought your tattoo to me."

Surveying the room, I saw nothing different about it or me. The sun tattoo lay quietly on my arm. But I remembered the flickering that distorted my vision, the images of Parker that had grown brighter, more distinct. The awful touch of Thutmose, with his greedy eyes.

"A beacon?"

"To the correct…," he paused, selecting his words, "Being, your presence is felt along the interlocking web of collective consciousness. Think of it like a pond. When your tattoo comes to life, it causes ripples that expand out to the edges of perception. Your underlying ability to sense emotion is honed more acutely each time the tattoo reacts, and it's your growing strength that's the issue."

"Issue?"

He set his beer bottle on the coffee table, careful to slide a coaster beneath it. "Not an issue with me. It puts you in danger from others. That's why I'm here."

My mind struggled to understand. Nothing made sense. "Which others?"

"You really don't know, do you?" He sighed and sat back on the couch.

"You said Parker's sense had been latent," I blurted out. "So both of us have this weird ability."

He nodded. "Not surprising. It's carried in the genetic code, but because it's recessive, it can skip a generation or two."

His information settled into place, explaining things I had puzzled over. If my brother and I both had the sense, it might mean the gene came down on my father's side. My father either had the sense, too, or was a carrier. Was that why he was so rigid? Fearful of what he could do or envious that we had it but he did not. "Who's after us? And why?"

"They're only after *you*," Pinscher said. "Or *maybe* after you. I don't know that you're in immediate danger, but the danger exists, and I had to let you know."

I thought of Khufu and his scarab. "I may have already had one run-in." I told him of the cult meeting, the overpowering smoke, the odd creature that had danced on the roof's edge. And the follow-up text.

Pinscher frowned. "Very troubling," he said. "They're moving faster than I expected."

A shiver went up my spine. "What do I do?"

Pinscher was about to speak when the doorbell rang. I jumped—Khufu on my doorstep, I was sure. We both stood.

"I'll do what I can to protect you," he said. "Know that you are becoming formidable yourself." He turned to the door, and I tensed, not sure what I faced or what was expected of me. "Relax," he said, once again smiling. "It's a friend."

Peering through the fisheye peephole, I saw Toby's face, felt his vibration through the door's wood, and sagged in relief. I had forgotten he was headed to my place.

Pulling open the door, I ushered him inside and offered introductions, while also scanning him for his status. I sensed curiosity, no blendered emotions.

"I've stayed too long," Pinscher said to me. "I'll leave you to your next guest."

I put a hand on his arm as he moved to the door. "You'll stay in touch?" He'd left me with a warning but no plan of action.

"Oh, yes." His eyes held mirth and the corners of his mouth turned up a bit. "I have my ways." He put his hand over mine. His palm was smooth, and his touch sent a calm that radiated through my entire body. "I've said before, and I fully believe it, trust in yourself, Quinn."

He closed the door behind him, and I was alone with Toby. We stood awkwardly for several moments, and then I led him to the living room couch. He sat, and for once, I sat there, too, but at the other end—not that my couch is enormous, but it gave me breathing room. I had no idea how this conversation would go.

I turned to sit facing him. "How is today?" I began, mentally crossing my fingers for his response.

"Touché," he said. "I deserve that. Today is a solid six."

Inwardly relaxing, I kept on my professional face. "And Eddi and your mother?"

"Both fine."

"Great." I looked at my watch. Past ten o'clock. "What's on your mind?"

He looked away and then at me. "I know I blew it with you, I let you down."

I shook my head vigorously. "You let *yourself* down. This is about you and your life, the way you put it back together. I'm only a bystander—someone who cares—but I can't do the work for you."

He spread his hands as though in supplication. "I'm totally clean now. When Braden showed up…" He sighed. "You're right. I can't blame him for what I did. He has his own demons to fight. It was my choice. And it's my choice now. To not go there again."

What had Pinscher said about my uber sense becoming more fine-tuned? I could sample the vibrations now, almost like a scientist assaying a specimen. I did this without thinking. Toby's were completely truthful.

"That's something to hold onto," I said. I reached forward to take his hands, and he pulled me into an embrace.

"I have waited so long to do this," he whispered in my ear. His lips found mine, and my body responded. I so wanted him.

But after a deeply passionate kiss, I gently pushed away. "Toby, we can't do this." Our faces were still close, too close, and I pushed farther. "I'm moved that you have feelings for me. And obviously I have feelings for you. But as I explained before, I can't ethically be in a relationship with you." I read disappointment in his face and felt sadness vibrating from him. It churned with the regret I was feeling. *If only…*

"I really fucked up, didn't I?" He was solemn. "If I'd stayed clean…"

Catching his meaning, I shook my head again. "That matters only to you and your recovery. It has no bearing on what you and I can or can't do."

He sighed and sat back on the couch. "Okay." I had feared an angry response, but I sampled nothing but continued disappointment.

"I'll be frank with you." I hesitated. Part of me wanted to say the hell with ethics. "If I wasn't your counselor…" I smiled. "We can still be friends—that's your call."

He stood, and I followed his lead, and we walked to the door. "It was worth a shot," he said, his own smile rueful. "If you ever change your mind…"

The morning staff meeting with Amanda Reed tried hard to be upbeat but failed. We went through the motions, discussed the problem cases, hailed the small victories, but there were few smiles around the table. Every second the clock ticked off was one second closer to the changing of the guard. Someone had put up a printout in the office kitchen of the new director's face. The caption, taped beneath it, read, *Would you trust this man with your paycheck?*

"All right, people," Amanda finally said. "Let's move 'em out."

It was her usual meeting tagline, something I once found irritating, but had grown to love. I would miss it.

My own office looked like the movers were due any moment. I had already cleared out my cabinets, shifting client files into designated boxes. My walls were bare, and I kept no framed family photos on my desk. Heywood had once remarked that my minimalist decor was a cover. What I really wanted, he said, was to prevent my clients from knowing who I was or what made me tick. He was absolutely right. My one concession to the emotional comfort of my clients was a small basket that held a variety of foam stress balls.

At five until noon, I picked up a green foam ball and compressed it on my way to Heywood's office. He picked up his lunch bag, and we headed to my condo to talk business.

He cranked up an oldies station on my radio. The Beatles sang of Sergeant Pepper, and Heywood beat out the rhythm on my dashboard.

I waited until the song ended, then turned down the volume. "I'm having second thoughts about this," I said. "About doing this from my house."

"I thought you might," he said, already switching rhythms to a Stones song.

"I didn't peg you for an oldies guy," I said.

He shook his head. "I just didn't connect with the pop stuff of the nineties. The oldies tunes have real meat on them, not that fluff of the Millennium."

"We'll agree to disagree on that," I said. "Metallica. Stone Temple Pilots. Soundgarden. That's real music." I held up my fist in the metal salute.

"Gaaaah!" Heywood hung his head out the window and pretended to puke.

At the condo, I gave him the tour, described Candi's vision for turning the extra bedroom into a clinical space, and shared my ideas about how to arrange our schedule for seeing clients.

"I like your plan, and the room will work if you convert it," Heywood said. He paced the living room. "Your place isn't all that far from mine, maybe ten minutes away."

I let him continue to pace while I fetched a yogurt from the fridge. "The pluses do add up," I said.

"But the minuses..." He sat at the table and unwrapped a sandwich he'd brought. "The biggest one besides will we bring in enough clients to support our business is, do you want strangers, especially those with shaky backgrounds, to have access to your home? I told you I wouldn't want that for myself. And frankly, if we're to be business partners, I will say as a partner, I don't want you to put yourself at risk. If something happens, our show goes down the tubes."

Spooning my yogurt, I knew I agreed. My special abilities might be getting better, sharper, but they wouldn't save my life if someone got violent. And both Heywood and I knew that was more than a possibility. The police were on speed dial at the office.

"Okay," I said. "Let's think about a Plan B."

The doorbell rang. I froze. This time, it really would be Khufu. The peephole showed a man about my age, dressed in street clothes. It wasn't Khufu, or FedEx or a postal delivery. He shifted one foot to the other. Scared, I read him.

I opened the door cautiously. Heywood seemed to sense my unease and placed himself nearby.

"Do I know you?" I said, holding the door only partially ajar.

"Braden sent me," the young man said, looking everywhere but at me. He took in Heywood standing behind me. "He said you were the best."

"At what?" I kept my voice gentle, not wanting to panic the stranger anymore than he already was.

"Detox," he said, wiping a hand across his face and finally looking directly at me. "I'm ready."

Chapter 26

Heywood and I stared at the young man. In response, he looked confused.

"You're Cutie, right?" He looked at the door frame, at my condo number. "Six twenty-one. Sunrise Court. It's where he said to go."

My brain processed the information. Cutie — *QT*, what Parker always called me. I opened the door fully. "Yes, I'm QT. Come in. And you are?"

"Matt." He stepped tentatively inside and looked at the foyer, the living room. "You do detox here?"

"Let's talk," I said. I brought him to the kitchen table and pulled out a chair. Heywood and I flanked him, but we both knew to soft pedal what we had to say.

"You've taken a huge step toward getting your life back," I said. "That first step is so hard, and you've done it. Heywood and I will help you find a place, but we are addiction counselors. We don't run a detox clinic here."

The news deflated Matt, and I sampled his mood. Fear, doubt. This was a crucial moment for him. The call of the dark side was strongest now, enticing him, when he faced a rough road.

"But Braden said..." His words drifted off.

"Braden is an old friend, and I appreciate what he was trying to do for you." I studied Matt, and something inside me shifted. " Let me make some calls right now. If there's nothing available, you're here, we'll make it work."

"Thomas," Heywood cut in. His look was of concern and surprise. "This is your *home*."

Matt put his hands on the table, his face haggard. "I've had enough of the shit. I want out. I just can't do it on my own because I'm too scared. But I'm not a coward."

"No one said you were," I said. "Let me get you a glass of water. Give me a sec."

Heywood followed me into the kitchen. "You can't do this here," he whispered. "It's too risky. You have no idea who this kid is."

I took a glass from a cabinet, added ice, and filled it with water. "I'll bet the Keystone Center has space. We'll get him in. And if they don't, what if you helped me? We're going to be partners, right?" I kept my voice low as well.

"This is exactly why setting up business here is a bad idea," he said, pacing again, but within the small confines of the kitchen. "This kid may work out fine, but what about the next one, the one who either needs medical intervention you can't give or turns on you—or me?"

He was right. This was a step neither of us was qualified to take, but I'd been caught off-guard. My first instinct was always to help—it's a big reason I went into counseling—but sometimes I forget to think of the consequences.

"I have a feeling about Matt—he'll be fine even if he has to stay here. But I'll concede that we need a Plan B for future clients." I carried the glass out to the table. "You'll need to stay hydrated," I said to Matt. "It will help you through this."

I went upstairs to call the detox center in private. No, they did not have any openings right then. Maybe in several weeks. I put Matt on the waiting list.

In the kitchen, I relayed the news and Heywood and I exchanged a glance, then I turned to Matt. "I'll put you up here for now."

Heywood headed to the office to finish out his day, and would return for the evening shift. "Promise me you'll call 911 if things go south," he said, as I walked him to the door.

I touched his sleeve. "I will. Thanks, Heywood."

He looked me up and down, wearing his usual sardonic grin. "Cutie? Maybe."

Matt and I settled in for what turned out to be a counseling session. A few moments in, I had a brief flash of panic, recalling Pinscher's warning of possible danger, but Matt's intentions were straightforward. He was younger than me by two years and had been in the grip of addiction since his late teens. His parents had thrown him out and he'd been living on friend's couches until they got tired of his using.

He turned over his car keys to me, and he emptied pockets and otherwise made sure he had nothing to tempt him during his withdrawal. My medicine cabinet held nothing stronger than regular Tylenol, so he wouldn't be pillaging there.

"Braden sent you, you said." I'd persuaded him to take a walk with me around the complex. Fluids and exercise can help the process, I'd said. "Is he okay?"

Matt shrugged. "I guess. He was talking about some sun god, spinning a story about how even after a thousand years, the god still had a hold of people."

I wanted to put Matt in my car, make him take me to Braden. Instead, I just nodded.

On the far side of the lot, we stepped onto the grass to let a car pass. It slowed to a crawl, and I blanched when I saw the driver. It was the man who called himself Ramses. He stared at me for a moment, then drove off.

They know where I live.

"Let's get back inside," I said to Matt.

Pushing my unease aside, I set Matt up with the TV and a handful of movies to keep his mind occupied. He didn't need to think about how scared he was to face what he faced. Matt had only been there a few hours, and already I was regretting my decision. What had I been thinking? And what if I'd put him in danger?

Moving my laptop to the kitchen table, I searched online for other places that I could send Matt. I made several more calls, but every place was full. When my phone buzzed, I hesitated to answer. Khufu? Ramses? It was my father.

"When you're done with work, come by." The last time I was there, he'd thrown me out. Apparently I was forgiven.

"How's Mom?" I deflected.

"Declining," he said. "But you knew that. The next time I call you will probably be to tell you that she's dead."

I closed my laptop and moved up to the bedroom, but left the door open so I could hear downstairs. Matt didn't need to listen to the never-ending war with my father.

"How are you doing, considering?" I kept my tone neutral, compassionate.

"Never better." His sarcasm ended with an unkind laugh.

"It's a tough time for you." I sank onto my bed. My mind slipped to worrying about Matt and the cult, but I redirected it to the issue at hand. "When the hospice nurse is there, you could give yourself a break, take a walk, go out for a bite to eat."

"Stop the counselor talk, Quinn," he said. "I'm not one of your addicts."

I reminded myself that grief had its stages and that anger was one of the first to hit. He was furious at my mother for dying and was taking it out on me.

"I'm just trying to help."

"The help I could use now is picking out a casket."

I sat up. "She doesn't want to be buried. She wants to be cremated. Her ashes scattered at the Jersey Shore."

He made a dismissive noise. "Once she's gone, it doesn't matter what she wants."

"It matters to her now. Those are her dying wishes." Damn my father for trying to control her on her deathbed—and beyond.

"Are you coming over or not?"

If I didn't go, he would buy the casket and blame me for it. If I did go, he would still buy the casket, just to spite me. In any case, I couldn't leave Matt until Heywood arrived to take the second shift.

"I'm waiting for a colleague. I'll be over once he shows up."

Heywood was as good as his word—even better. He brought pizza and soda and waved off my guilt at needing to leave for my parents'. "Go. We'll be fine. Amanda is trying to pull some strings for us, to get Matt a bed somewhere." He winked. "You'd better be back before the Phils game starts. They're playing the Dodgers at ten."

I tried to be lighthearted to match his mood, but failed. "Be careful while I'm out."

Heywood reacted to my expression and lowered his voice. "I'm always careful. Why?"

I couldn't explain without sounding paranoid, so I said lamely, "Just because."

My father allowed me into his study, where his computer sat. The room had been off-limits when I was a child, and even as an adult, crossing the room's threshold made me uneasy. I expected a reprimand.

And as an adult taking in the room, I felt slightly disappointed, as well. It was smaller than I'd remembered, no mysteries hidden in the corners. Instead, the desk, the chairs, the lone bookcase were of simple, modest lines. Wood, a bit of chrome. He had almost no trinkets on display—just like me. In all, an orderly room reflecting the orderliness of his engineer's mind.

He had been searching online for funeral information. The page displayed was a website for McLaren's Funeral Home, a local establishment.

"They'll do a funeral with a casket and burial, or they'll handle cremation," he said, all business. "I have an appointment with them on Thursday. You can take the afternoon off to come with me."

My knee-jerk reaction was anger, but I squelched it. I owed it to my mother to fight for what she wanted.

"Sure," I said. "What about the church? Have you talked to the pastor about a service?"

He settled into his chair and steepled his fingers, the irony lost on him. "Pastor Kent advised me to follow Sonia's preference on that. She wants a memorial service instead of a funeral."

No surprise that the pastor's word carried more weight than mine. At least we were in agreement—and he didn't even know me.

"That sounds fine, Dad."

"He'll work with me to set a date and time once…" My father looked away. I felt the vibration of his grief envelope me. His just-business facade fell away.

"Can I see Mom? I won't stay long, just a minute to peek in on her."

He frowned, but nodded. "I'll come with you. She's very fragile, hardly ever awake when I'm sitting with her."

We walked into the darkened bedroom. As though protecting her from anything disruptive I might dream up, my father stood close to the bed. The vibrations from her were slow, even, calm. No pain rippled out, and I was thankful. I kissed her gently on the forehead, but she didn't stir. This, I knew, was the last time I would see her, touch the warmth of her skin, be able to whisper in her ear that I loved her.

In the hallway, my father walked me to the front door.

"She's not in pain," I said. "I'm glad for that."

"It's the medication they're giving her." He looked away again. "The nurse says that soon she'll stop eating, not that she's eating much now. That will be the end."

I wanted to give him a hug, to reassure him, but my father would refuse it. A handshake was as much touch as he could tolerate and that seemed too formal, so I did nothing. Just waited until he'd recovered and opened the door.

There, on the front porch, Braden knelt, playing tug with Gideon. He looked up when the door opened.

"Mr. Thomas," he said, dropping the dog toy and standing. He wouldn't meet my eye. "About Mrs. Thomas—Quinn told me. I'd like to see her, to say goodbye."

"She's not up for visitors," he said brusquely. "And it's already evening. Maybe some other time."

"Dad—" I started.

"No," he said. "I won't have an addict in my home."

Braden, who vibrated with anxiety and panic, wasn't high at that moment. "You've never liked me, maybe you even hated me because of Parker, but I won't hurt you."

"You couldn't hurt me, Brady," my father said, using a nickname I remembered Braden hated. "You're a spineless excuse for a human being."

"Dad, stop!" I said. "Leave him alone."

My father stepped out onto the porch, shutting the door, not giving Braden any chance to slip around him and into the house.

"That you, a young woman, have to defend your worthless male friend, who can't fight his own fights, proves my point."

That's when Braden punched my father in the face.

Chapter 27

Even the skinny, undernourished body of a drug user can pack a wallop if it lands right. My father yelped at the blow, and blood flowed from his nose. Braden's fist had connected with enough power to throw my father off balance. He back-stepped, flailing until he managed to grab the porch rail.

Braden cradled his fist in his other hand. "Ow, ow," he muttered.

My mother, who once had been the peacemaker in a similar face-off between Parker and my father, was not in any shape to intervene. That now fell to me.

"Enough," I said, not raising my voice but lasering it. I felt my own vibrations expand outward and in strength. *I am a wall*, I thought. *A firebreak.* Neither Braden nor my father could move an inch toward each other even if they wanted to.

"You're doing that?" Braden said.

Yes. I thrust the answer into his mind. Then I retracted the flow and turned to my father. The anger of a moment before had been replaced with a deep exhaustion. "Let's go inside and I'll get you a cool cloth and some ice." To Braden, I said softly, "Go see my mom, but just for a minute. She's pretty zoned out."

My father allowed me to guide him into the bathroom. I sat him on the toilet seat, found an ice pack in the freezer, and worked to clean him up. He was silent, but not brooding, just there—as though Braden's punch had knocked more than his nose askew.

I'd placed a small bandage on his nose and was rinsing the blood out of the washcloth when he revived. His eyes focused on me.

"What are you?" he said.

"I'm your daughter." It was the simplest answer. I wiped out the sink and hung up the cloth. "Do you feel like lying down?"

By the time I helped my father to his own bed in my old room and closed and locked the front door behind me, Braden was back on the porch.

"Thanks for letting me in," he said. "Your mom…"

"Yeah." I sat on the step, and after a beat, he sat beside me. "She doesn't have long."

He looked out to the street, quiet, but the underlying frantic vibrations told me he was fighting to hold it together.

"I'm sorry I hit your dad. I hope he doesn't press charges or anything."

"Apology accepted, even if he deserved it. He's such as ass." I wanted to hug Braden. "I was worried about you. You saved my life and then vanished."

He continued to stare out at the darkening street. "I couldn't stay. It was my fault."

"It was my fault for insisting we go. I was so sure I could handle whatever came my way. If you hadn't rescued me..." I reached out and took his hand. He flinched but then relaxed. I intertwined my fingers with his. "So you followed me here. Any particular reason—beyond my mom?"

His shoulders slumped, and he looked out at the street. In the dimming light of the evening sky, I could see a tear glistening in his eye. "Some days I think I can live with this," he said. "You've found a way. The strength I felt flowing from you on the porch..."

Know that you are becoming formidable yourself.

I was just powerful enough to get myself killed, if I wasn't careful.

"You heard my dad. That was my childhood. I wondered why I was cursed." I squeezed his hand. "I know now that I am what I am, and so are you. Different, yes. Evil, no. Strong, yes. You. Are. Strong."

We sat for several minutes in silence, until my cell phone rang. It was Heywood.

"Are you okay?" he said, his voice strained.

"I'll live," I said. "Is it Matt? Is he in trouble?"

"No." He paused. "But you need to get back here as soon as you can. Weird stuff."

Weird? Ramses or Khufu or some other fake pharaoh must have shown up. "I'm on my way." I turned to Braden. "Come with me. We'll figure it out together."

He shook his head. "I can't. Maybe I'll stop by later."

I hoisted my backpack and gave him a hug. "I'll be waiting."

He hugged me tightly and whispered, "I love you, QT." Then he walked to his car and drove off.

"Finally," Heywood snapped, when I walked through my condo door.

He was awash in panic, but Matt was snoozing on the couch.

"What's wrong?" I said. I set my backpack on a chair. The room looked exactly as I'd left it, even down to the open pizza boxes and dirty plates on the table. "Is it Matt?"

"Did you see the guy?" Heywood said as though he hadn't heard me. "Short. Kind of round. Dangerous eyes."

Not a cult member. I relaxed. Heywood had to be overreacting.

"Where?" I said, stepping farther into the room. I looked around and moved toward the kitchen.

"Not in here," Heywood said, with exasperation. "He was at the door maybe half an hour ago, looking for you. I thought maybe he was still hanging around outside."

"He spooked you." It wasn't a question. It explained the panic coming from Heywood. "Was it another client looking for detox?"

"No." Heywood was emphatic. "I was worried that somehow he'd waylaid you. And then you didn't answer your phone."

Checking it, I saw the missed calls. And a text from an unknown number. *it is time.*

"Sorry," I said, now unnerved myself. "Looks like all but that last one went straight to voicemail."

"He said, 'Tell her we know.'" Heywood studied me. "Thomas, what does that mean?"

You shine like a beacon, Pinscher had said. *To the right 'being.'*

"It means I need to be careful," I said.

"You said that before you left—be careful. What the hell are you mixed up in?"

"It doesn't involve you. It's nothing about counseling or detox or any of that." I needed to be extra careful that everyone in my circle stayed safe. "I'll be fine. Go cheer the Phils." I put a smile on my face and pushed him to the door.

"Matt's doing fine," Heywood said. "He'll make it. Then comes the rest of his life."

I peered outside the door as Heywood strode to his car. Nothing odd. I felt no threatening emotion close by. But I closed the door, locked it, and threw the deadbolt.

What had the text meant? It was time for what?

With Matt still peacefully asleep, I cleared the rest of the table mess. In less than fifteen minutes, the kitchen was tidy. Candi would have been proud.

I pulled the novel I'd started off the stack, and finally fell under its spell for at least an hour. Matt stirred on the couch and sat up. I brought him more water to drink. His face was pale but his teeth no longer chattered.

"How long has it been?" he said. "My whole body aches."

"You've almost made it a whole day," I said. "This is the toughest part."

Matt yawned and settled on the couch. Prowling through the condo, I checked every window and made sure the front door was dead bolted. Whatever weird occurrence had spooked Heywood had not shown up again, but I was taking no chances. I grabbed a pillow and another blanket, made myself comfortable in the living room, and read until my eyes fluttered closed.

At sunrise, I checked on Matt and set the coffeemaker to brew in thirty minutes, while I showered and made breakfast. By the morning light, the world seemed much less threatening.

By the time I put plates on the table, Matt was awake and ravenous. Scrambled eggs, toast, and slices of cantaloupe disappeared in the time it took me to eat my yogurt.

"What happens next?" Matt said.

"If you mean right now, you're free to use the shower. After that, it's up to you—rest, TV, read, take a walk with me. My boss is still trying to get you into official detox. You're still several days out from the end of the physical symptoms."

"And then?"

I looked him in the eye. "It's the first day of the rest of your life." I stood to clear the table. "Each day you move beyond your detox is one more day in your sobriety account. The days become weeks become months become years." I handed him the plates. "It takes work. Let's go load the dishwasher."

We spent the rest of the day trying different distractions. When TV turned boring, I hauled out a few board games a friend had given me. We walked around the complex. I read aloud from a Neil Gaiman short story. We played a fantasy card game.

Heywood checked in several times by phone.

"No weird visitors," I assured him.

A detox center from the next county over called in mid-afternoon, with an opening for Matt. He could check in the following morning.

"They're equipped to help you no matter what you go through," I told Matt after hanging up. "You're off to a great start, though."

I texted Candi to make plans for a training ride. We could do sprints and discuss race strategy.

Be by at 4, she replied. Heywood promised to drop by at 4, too, to relieve me.

When the doorbell rang a little before 4, I was dressed to ride, my bike leaning against the wall, my helmet dangling from a handlebar by its strap. I pulled open the door, flipping a mental coin to guess if it was Heywood or Candi.

It was neither.

A short, rather round man slipped past me, through the doorway. I stumbled and gasped as my tattoo seared my arm.

Chapter 28

It was the same small man who had beckoned me on the Philly rooftop. He took a few steps into the condo, but immediately turned to me. He was no taller than my chest, the height of a ten-year-old maybe, but his eyes spoke of agelessness—and something else less benign.

"What do you want?" I said. It was difficult to concentrate with my arm on fire. I tried to sample his intent but it was as though he was enveloped in a bubble. It was the first time I'd felt nothing from a person, even by consciously trying.

"You," the man said.

That struck me as enormously funny even knowing he was dead serious. "Sorry, you can't have me," I said and laughed. "You tried to lure me before, and it didn't work." When he didn't react, I added, raising my voice, "Get out, now."

"You will come with me," he said.

Candi arrived on my doorstep, and although I motioned for her to stop, she walked in anyway, with her bike, joining the person I had mentally tagged as Mr. Odd. She seemed to grasp the situation and, after parking her bike, positioned herself near me.

"I'm not going anywhere with you," I told him. "I don't know who you are or what you want."

"Parker," he said.

As quickly as my reaction surfaced, I buried it.

"Parker," Candi said. "That's your name?" She played along with me.

Then Heywood was at the door, pulling it open with one hand, juggling a bag with the other.

"Dinner," he announced, but stopped when he saw the crowded foyer. "This is the guy, the one who showed up for you yesterday."

Mr. Odd ignored both of them and kept his eyes on me. "Parker," he said again and stepped closer, reaching a hand out to me.

I retreated, but I had only a few feet before I would run into the wall.

Shuffling in from the living room, Matt walked right up to Mr. Odd. "No, you don't," Matt said. He reached his own hands out to stop the man.

In that instant, everything froze. Matt, Candi, Heywood, all ceased moving, as though someone had taken a photo and that's what I was looking at.

Mr. Odd, however, was still advancing toward me. I knew that if he touched me, I would indeed be going with him, an outcome I would not like. I stepped back another foot, relieved that I could still move. *Think,* I told myself. *Quickly.*

A faint image of Pinscher flickered in my mind. Remember, his voice murmured. And I did. Once again, I pushed my vibrations out, expanding them beyond my physical being. This time, instead of stopping Braden and my father, I pushed toward the creature only inches away. *I am a shield,* I thought.

The man/creature recoiled as though touched by something too hot, emitting a howl that hurt my ears. I pushed harder, and *he* retreated this time, and in the instant it took me to blink my eyes, he was gone.

Breathing deeply, I tried to relax. My tattoo was once again quiet, but only one prominence remained. *Extraordinary,* Pinscher's presence whispered just inside my ear.

I allowed myself a smile.

The three others in my foyer burst into movement as though a switch had tripped somewhere.

"Thomas," Heywood said, with a shout, dropping the bag with dinner and rushing toward me.

Candi looked first in the foyer and then out the door. "Where is he?"

Matt put his hands in the pockets of his jeans and looked at me. "I think I'm in the home stretch after that."

"He was here, you all froze, and then he vanished," I said. The look Candi gave me said, *Bullshit.* I didn't care. I was suddenly starving. "Dinner's arrived. Let's eat."

Over hoagies, we speculated about Mr. Odd. Heywood was sure he was an evil Hobbit. Matt pegged him as a member of a small mob.

"No," Candi said, waving a spear of dill pickle, "he was definitely an alien."

"The real question is, why was he here?" Heywood said. "Why you, Thomas?"

"And why did he ask about Parker?" Candi added.

The three of them fell silent, waiting for my answer.

"The cult," I finally said. "He was there. Not for long, but he was there, beckoning me to join him on the roof's edge."

"Jesus, Thomas," Heywood said. "This is about your brother, right?"

"It seems so."

"Then I'll tell you what you told me—be careful." Heywood was more agitated than I'd ever seen him.

I put on a pretend smile. "Of course." I stood to clear my plate. "But right now I need to get some miles in. Candi, are you still up for a ride?"

She smiled wanly. "I guess."

I strapped on my helmet. "We'll be fine. I'd stake our sprints against any alien in the universe." I tried to keep my tone light.

Heywood handed me my pepper spray. "If you have to go, then be well armed."

"Pepper spray and psychic power. I can't lose," I quipped. I wished I felt as confident as my words.

I was at the door when Candi called, "Wait." She had stopped short on her way through the living room. "There, on the bookshelf." She pointed to the astrolabe. "It's come back."

On the towpath, Candi and I traded off the lead, doing sprints, until we'd ridden fifteen miles. At the turnaround, we took a water break and assessed our chances in the race. It was only a few days away.

"You've been training harder than me," Candi said. "You'll rock."

"The real athletes will be smoking the route. I'll be happy to beat my old time by a few minutes." I wiped my face with a bandanna. "If I can concentrate enough to finish."

Candi took another swig from her water bottle. "How are you feeling, really? Your mom, your work, this weird shit going down with your brother—it's a lot. And you keep a lot hidden."

My eyes smarted. "You know me too well." I sighed. "On the inside, I'm a wreck."

"One way or another, things are going to change soon," she said. "May they go your way."

"That's what scares me the most." I snugged my helmet and got ready to roll. "That nothing will."

She smiled. "No matter what, you've still got your friends. I'll be there for you." She sped ahead to lead the way.

We sprinted the last half mile of the towpath and then dialed it back to low until we were at the condo. I thought Candi would head on to her own place, but she lingered.

I guessed at her motive. "It's the astrolabe, isn't it?"

"I just want a chance to try it," she said. "Do you mind?"

The last time we'd been interrupted by Braden. "Nope," I said. "But it'll be a while before the sky's dark enough."

Inside, in the kitchen, I handed her a bottled iced tea, and when she raised her eyebrows, I pointed to Matt, on the couch, immersed in a movie, an old '80s flick with Robert DeNiro. "No alcohol while he's here," I said. "He doesn't need any temptations." I'd sent my beer stash home with Heywood, who promised to keep it for me—or not, he'd joked.

When the movie ended, the four of us played hearts until the sky had become sufficiently dark for stars to appear. Carrying the astrolabe, Candi led Heywood, Matt, and me to the far edge of the parking lot, away from the lot's lights.

"Just like last time, we'll use Vega as our reference point," she said, pointing to the glimmering speck overhead. "It's part of the Summer Triangle."

"Like you, me, and Cutie?" Matt said with a chuckle.

Heywood laughed out loud.

Candi can charm the pants off—well, just about every guy she meets.

"You wish!" she said. But she asked him to hold the penlight while she found Vega on the front of the astrolabe. "Here," she pointed. "Now I move the rete until it lines up with Vega's altitude."

"Cool," Matt said. "How do you know all this?"

Candi's smile widened. "I had one years ago. This one's even better." She moved another piece on the astrolabe. As she did, my sun tattoo activated, not searing my arm as it had earlier in the presence of Mr. Odd, but throbbing. I placed my hand over it.

"There," she said. "According to this, the time is 8:54." She frowned. "But that's off an hour."

Over her shoulder, Parker's image shifted into view, strengthening and solidifying. It was the strongest image yet, as though I could reach out and touch him. I felt no emotions from him, but so vivid was his face that I could see the deep sadness in his gaze.

Heywood and Matt bent over the astrolabe with Candi. "Has to be daylight savings," Matt said.

"Of course!" Candi said. "I should have thought of that."

They continued to banter while I stared at Parker.

Come home, I said to him, in my thoughts.

Keep your guard up, QT, he said. *It's not what you think.*

"I don't know what to think," I whispered aloud. "But I know you're in trouble. You wanted my help—and now you don't?"

Forget about me and go live your own life.

I took a step toward his image. "That would be like forgetting my name. It's not going to happen. We're family."

He continued to gaze at me, and I took in his gaunt frame, the tangled beard, the hollowness in his eyes. Where was the Parker who'd painted those magnificent murals, the brother who wrote me faithfully despite my never answering a line?

"I don't care what it costs," I said. "I'll find you."

He closed his eyes and recited:

Where you hold me enchain'd a certain time, refusing to give me up

His image flickered and died away.

"No," I said, biting my lip to keep from crying.

"Who are you talking to?" Heywood said.

Candi took one look at my face, handed the astrolabe to Matt, and gave me a hug. "Her brother," she said. "He shows up randomly but isn't ever quite there."

"He was so close, so real…" I wiped the back of my hand across my eyes.

"Parker was here?" Heywood said, scanning the darkened field.

"For just a few moments," I said, trying not to let my voice quaver. "That's all I ever seem to get. Then he's gone."

The next afternoon I met my father at the funeral home he'd selected. We looked at caskets, and when my father didn't get the hint after I cleared my throat for the third time, I spoke up.

"Can we also see the urns?" I said.

My father glared at me briefly but then nodded at the salesman. "My wife wants to be cremated and her ashes scattered."

After a discussion about cremation and urn styles, my father surprised me by asking me which one to choose. Any of them would have done, but I pointed to the dark gray, modest but in a color my mother favored.

My father was signing the paperwork, finishing the contract, when I felt a surge of grief well up in me. I was sad, yes, but this seemed deeper, more powerful than just contemplating my mother's passing. My father didn't seem perturbed by anything at that moment. I shook it off as delayed reaction to the formalities of the funeral home process.

On my way to the condo, though, my phone buzzed.

My father, by then at home, said only four words and then ended the call. "It's over. She's gone."

Gripping the steering wheel with extra force, I blinked back the tears that sprang up. This was the expected outcome of the last few months, but the reality of her death hit me harder than I anticipated. *She's no longer hurting*, I told myself.

"Bullshit!" I shouted aloud, in the car. Empty platitudes like that were no balm. They just made it worse.

I had the answer before I pulled into the condo lot. I would ride the race that weekend in memory of my mother.

But Fate had another surprise for me. The door to my condo was unlocked. I froze in the doorway, my hand still on the latch. Had Mr. Odd returned? I sampled the room beyond, and sensed a slow churning.

"Hello?"

With no answer, I stepped further in. I'd driven Matt to the detox facility that morning. It couldn't be him. "Who's there?"

I still heard nothing. But that sluggish churning—where was it coming from? Still numb from the news of my mother's passing, I tried to think. An image tugged at me, from the parking lot, a familiar bumper sticker. *Adjust Your Altitude.*

Panic surged through me then and I raced into the living room. On the couch, which had seen so much use over the last month or two, lay Braden. One arm was draped across Parker's sketchbook, and the other hung limply to the carpet. His eyes were closed, his breathing so shallow I could barely see his chest move. His pulse was faint.

"No, no!" I shouted, shaking him. "You can't do this, Braden!"

He did not respond.

I called 911 and knelt beside him. "Hang in there," I said, feeling helpless. I had nothing else to offer until the ambulance arrived. "Parker," I whispered, my hand on the sun tat, willing it to connect. "Save him, please."

Instead, I heard Pinscher's voice murmur, as though from a long distance. *Trust in yourself.*

With a vision blurred by tears, I grasped Braden's hand and placed it over my heart. "You will not die," I said fiercely, sending whatever energy I could from me to him.

It seemed I had closed my eyes for just a heartbeat, no longer than a second, and the EMT crew was pushing through the door.

Chapter 29

The ventilator cycled—breath in, breath out. Its endless, slow repetition overlay the accelerated beep of the heart monitor. Braden was as still as I'd found him in my condo. The ICU nurse hovered near me, and once again I felt helpless.

"I'm sorry, but your time is up," the nurse said. "You'll have to leave now."

I placed my hand gently on Braden's arm and leaned forward to whisper in his ear. "You. Are. Strong."

No response.

In the waiting area, I took the same green chair I'd been sitting on for the last two hours. Mrs. Hewitt glanced my way and went back to her magazine. I'd followed the ambulance to All Saints Medical Center, and represented myself as Braden's counselor, which was more or less true. I had called Mrs. Hewitt to let her know what had happened. She had barely spoken to me since arriving except to hiss, "You made this happen."

Whatever Braden had taken had almost put him under for good, the emergency doctor told me. He was intubated to keep his airway open, but his heart was still going a bit haywire. He would stay in ICU until he was able to breathe on his own.

Was it intentional? I'd asked. My gut said yes.

"If he makes it, you'll have to ask him," the doctor said. "Because of the circumstances, when he's out of ICU, we may need to keep him for a few days to make sure he's stable."

My body felt heavy, weary, as though I'd run ten miles, yet I couldn't sit still.

Candi texted me as I paced. *Still going to ride tomorrow?*

Yes, I texted. Even if I came in last, I would ride the race for my mother and for Braden. It would give me something to focus on besides the guilt I felt. How had I not seen this coming?

Get some sleep, if u can.

I sent a smiley face. Insomnia, my frequent friend, had plenty of encouragement that day to hang around. But she was right—I did need rest.

The elevators opened and Heywood walked onto the floor.

"Hey," I said, touched that he was there.

"I'm sending you home."

"Gotta stay," I yawned. "Gotta keep him alive."

"You've passed the torch to me, whether you agree or not." He handed me my backpack. "Get out of here and go ride your race. He's in fine hands."

I stood and slipped the backpack onto my shoulder, then gave him a hug. "You're a good man."

When I turned to the elevator, he winked. "That's a start, Thomas. Keep those hugs coming." Then sober-faced again, he added, "I'll let you know how he's doing."

At the condo, sleep, as I predicted, would not come. The place was too quiet, too empty after the revolving door of guests and crashers I'd had. In an endless replay, I saw Braden, unconscious and tethered to a machine, holding on — maybe.

Finally, at five after five, I gave up, dressed in my riding gear, a black band around my left arm, and ate an early breakfast. I was picking up Candi and her bike at seven.

On the couch where I'd found Braden less than twenty-four hours earlier, I opened up the sketchbook and studied the pages. This was my brother's amazing artwork, but it was also Braden's likeness. He had held to his promise to keep the sketchbook safe. *It's my lifeline,* he'd said.

A slip of paper fell out from between the pages, and I picked it up off the floor. Addressed to me, Braden's note was short. *Fortes fortuna iuvat.*

The phrase both Khufu and Pinscher had used. Fortune favors the brave.

Braden had added in his careful printing, *You are the bravest person I know.*

That was a lie. I was the biggest coward.

The thing about a race that's not really a race — you do your best and try not to think about the true athletes who will finish the course well ahead of you. Maybe hours ahead.

Candi and I buckled on our helmets. We had our water bottles. The day, a day before the official solstice, had clear skies and a slight breeze. Forecast high was in the upper 70s. Fifty miles through rolling countryside, a large loop beginning and ending at West Chester. I'd ridden this route every year for the last five years, a way to mark Parker's birthday. Candi and I always

148

toasted to him at the end with a bottle of champagne I had chilling in a cooler in my car.

This year, I'd left the champagne at home.

"See you at the end," Candi said, blowing a kiss my way. "Rock the road for them!" She was trying her best to keep the mood light, but her eyes betrayed her.

The starting gun sounded, and the mass of cyclists surged forward. Within minutes, the pack was strung out, with the speedsters pulling far ahead, and the middling riders settling into a rhythm they hoped would carry them through the miles.

My rhythm turned to *Bra-den So-nia*. Each pedal round repeated one of their names. Spiked with adrenalin, I pushed myself, coasting down the hills, but powering on the upgrades. My focus narrowed to the asphalt, my tires, the road sounds of the other cyclists near me. My concentration kept my feelings walled off. I didn't have to think about living or dying, love or fear.

Panting up a particularly steep grade, I heard another cyclist gradually overtaking me. It was a woman maybe ten years older than me.

"Looking good," she called over. "Your arm band. Who're you riding for?"

I told her, and although she was already inching ahead, she eased back slightly until she was alongside, both of us pumping and puffing. We kept climbing in sync until we reached the crest of the hill.

She gave a kind of half salute. "I'll ride for them too," she said, sliding ahead again. "Double the karma."

When I blasted through Phoenixville, I spotted Toby and Eddi on the right, Eddi on his shoulders. "You got this!" Toby yelled, and Eddi clapped.

Forty-five miles is almost fifty, I told myself later. My legs burned from the lactic acid building in the muscles, but I pedaled on. The end was so near, and according to the time stamp on a bank along the route, I was going to beat any past time by much more than a few minutes. We're talking a half hour. I felt jubilant and then immediately guilty for that. I wasn't supposed to be happy that day. I was in mourning.

It was on a curve outside Downingtown, my stamina waning, when I cut too close to the edge of the shoulder. The edge filled with loose gravel. To avoid it, I swerved, and fatigue slowed my reflexes enough that I went over, hitting the pavement and sliding.

"Fuck!" I cried out.

Two cyclists stopped for me. One helped me stand and brushed off the debris from my legs. The other rescued my bike, giving it a once over.

"Looks like you bent a rim," cyclist number two said. "Bummer. We're only a few miles from the finish."

They both sped off, after confirming that I had nothing broken. I could wait for the sag wagon or I could walk my bike. Even if I couldn't finish on two wheels, I had to cross the finish line. I started walking, the front wheel wobbling slightly.

Candi caught up with me about ten minutes later.

"You okay?" she said, slowing to pedal beside me.

When I'd told her about the crash and the bent rim, she dismounted to walk.

"Go on," I said. "I'll be fine."

"Take my bike," she said. "Finish this, for them."

The look she gave me said I wasn't to argue.

I'm taller than Candi, not by much but enough that pedaling her bike threw off my usual cadence. It took me half a mile to settle into a steady pace. My right knee twinged from the fall and skid, and my elbow and lower arm leaked blood from the road burn.

Upgrade, downgrade, shifting to make it easier on my knee, I covered the last few miles more slowly than I'd hoped. It was better than walking, though.

The streamers and balloons ahead marked the end, and I coasted across the line, my fist raised in victory. Even with the delay from the crash, I had beat my best time by eleven minutes. But that achievement didn't change the sad facts in my life. My mother was still gone. And Braden was still walking the fine line between life and death.

Chapter 30

The sag wagon picked up Candi, and together we sped to my place to change clothes, eat a quick meal, and drive to the hospital. Braden had been moved out of ICU and onto a general floor.

Outside Braden's room, Mr. Hewitt was chatting with a nurse. When he saw me, he broke off and faced me, arms folded across his chest. He was vibrating with anger and sadness. I couldn't blame him.

"How is he?" I said, Candi at my elbow, trying to see around Mr. Hewitt into the room.

"Holding his own finally," he said.

"Can we see him?" I remembered Braden's words as we sat on my parents' porch steps. *Some days I think I can live with this.* I had to help him change that to *every day.*

"I think you've done enough damage," Mr. Hewitt said.

"She saved his fucking life," Candi said. "And she just rode her bike fifty miles for him."

I held up a hand to hush her. "It's okay. We're all upset."

Emerging from the room, Mrs. Hewitt saw me and frowned, but then nodded. "He's asking for you." She turned to her husband. "Roy, we're going to let her. He's adamant."

Candi pushed me forward. "You go. I'll stay here."

The room, with one empty bed, was dim, the lights turned low. Braden was in the far bed, his face hollowed out by exhaustion. I felt the slow beat of it. He was breathing on his own, but still hooked to an IV. His blue eyes took me in, though, and his mouth turned up in a slight smile.

"You came," he said, his voice raspy from the ventilator.

I hugged him as best I could without tangling in the lines. "I was at the ICU, but you were out of it." I perched on the stuffed chair at his bedside.

"Yeah," he said. "I don't remember much, except…" He let his words drift off.

"I found your note. I should have known—you were calling out for help and I missed it. I let you down." The tears I had kept at bay since the previous night threatened to spill out.

"I was trying to bring him back," he said. "If you could summon him, I thought I could too." He frowned in concentration. "Especially if I helped the process along."

"And you overdid it."

"Yeah." He lapsed into silence for a few moments. "I meant it—what I wrote," he said.

"Of course you did. I know that—even if you're wrong. You're the brave one now."

"Can you be brave enough for both of us?" He sighed. "I'm just so fucking tired of it all."

"We'll be brave together. I'll be by your side every step of the way, if you'll let me." And I meant it.

"After what I've done to you? Breaking into your place, trying to stab you, then nearly getting you killed on that rooftop." He shook his head slightly, the effort seemed to exhaust him.

"You saved my life. You owe me nothing—except your honesty."

He cried then, and I held his hand, once again intertwining my fingers in his. When I left him for the evening, his parents were civil to me. He would be admitted to inpatient detox and rehab. They understood its importance and actually looked to me for advice.

Candi insisted that I stay at her place, and I didn't take much convincing. The adrenaline that had coursed through me for the last two days left me with my own deep exhaustion.

"I'm ordering take out," she said.

"I think I just want to sleep." I yawned. "Another early day tomorrow."

"You look like shit, Quinn, but you have to eat."

My eyes were closing on their own, determined that I would snooze that night. Then the doorbell rang, and I jerked myself awake.

"Don't open the door," I said.

Candi hushed me. "I invited him over for dinner. I hope you don't mind."

It was Toby, who beamed when he saw me, his right hand holding a small bouquet of daisies.

"Eddi chose these," he said, handing the flowers to me.

"Thanks for cheering me on," I said. "You and Eddi." I wanted to snuggle up next to him and doze, but stopped myself.

He must have sensed my decision because he chose a seat across from the couch where I sprawled. "Braden's doing okay?"

I smiled. "He's going to make it."

"Thanks to you, I heard," he said.

"I owed him one." I yawned again.

When the doorbell rang a second time, Toby rose to answer it and returned with two bags worth of food.

With fish tacos on the table, I marshaled my strength to sit and eat. Toby's bulk to my left made it easy for me to inch my chair closer and lean on him. I knew I shouldn't, but I thought, my life may end tomorrow, so I really didn't care.

"You've got quite a museum here," Toby said to Candi. He gestured at the faux torch lamp over the table, the battle shields hanging in the living room, the longsword behind me on the wall.

Candi grinned. "Medieval is my middle name. I was born in the wrong century."

He nodded and slid another taco onto his plate. "And it's all real?"

"No. The real stuff belongs in museums," Candi said between bites. "But that sword's a real enough replica. I'm bringing it with us tomorrow."

My chest clenched. Khufu and gang. I'd conveniently put them out of my mind. "You think they'll show?"

"Who?" Toby asked.

I hesitated to say it aloud, as though speaking the words would invoke their presence.

Candi filled in the answer when I stayed silent. "The sun cult." She pulled the longsword from its hanger and stepped away from the table to swing it.

Toby reached out for the sword. "Can I?"

She turned it over to him, and he too swung it to feel the heft.

"You're stronger than you look," Toby said. "This thing's not light."

Candi laughed, taking the sword from him. "Thanks. They'll have to fight off me and my Round Table friends. I invited a few of them."

"I'll be there too," Toby said. "Nobody gets past me."

I was touched. "Thanks, both of you." A wave of exhaustion washed over me. "I've got to call it a day."

Toby put his arm around me and pulled me close. "Sleep well. You'll see—you'll get your brother back."

For the second day in a row, I was up before dawn, this time my legs aching from the race. My energy level was keying to a fever pitch. I wanted to have it all be over—the goal seemed so far-fetched I wondered why I had ever thought it possible.

I made coffee and rummaged in Candi's cabinets to find two travel mugs. I wore my owl pendant and brought the astrolabe, for good luck. Candi and I picked up Toby and headed to Chester County, to find the Brandywine Notch.

On the winding road along the Brandywine Creek, we looked for a small pull-off. A graveled shoulder, the directions said.

Ahead, four or five vehicles were parked on the edge of the road, with no room for my car.

"This has to be the spot," Candi said.

I drove into the grass, hoping that later, the tires would grip enough to get us onto the asphalt.

The three of us threaded through a strand of barbed wire across a narrow dirt path that led up an incline. Trees and bushes flanked the path, but at the top, where the cloudless sky was lightening, the trees gave way to meadow.

"Up there," I said to Candi and Toby. They followed me single-file on the path. The air was thick with morning dampness, and I tasted sycamore on the slight breeze.

Ten minutes later, we emerged from the trees and could see an outcropping of stone ahead and farther up. The path widened and now cut through a field of wildflowers. Topping the ridge, I halted. The granite outcropping was a jumble of large stones. Near the base, several people stood. They carried colorful banners and were singing a song I didn't recognize.

The important detail about the Notch, Candi's research found, was the timing. The solstice sun would stream through the Notch a few minutes after seven—the exact time no one seemed to know. Maybe it varied from year to year; she wasn't sure. My watch said 6:51.

"What do we do now?" Toby asked.

I pointed to the small gathering. "We wait with them."

The median age of the half-dozen people standing near the rock formation seemed to be fifty or maybe even sixty. Hold-overs from a Woodstock generation, I guessed.

One of the people in the group waved us over.

"Here for the solstice Notch?" the woman said. Her gray hair was braided with flowers.

Yes, I told her. But it was also my brother's birthday. He'd been missing for ten years.

Her look was full of pity, and the vibrations she gave off reflected that. "Some say the Notch can bring change," she said, her tone kindly. "It's never happened for me, but who knows, maybe today is for you." She pointed out the Notch, a slit in one of the rocks a head or more above us.

Heywood scrambled up the path to join the group. "I thought I would miss it," he said. Following him, five or six others crested the hill. They were outfitted in Medieval costumes and they carried their own banners.

"Hey there," Candi called and went to meet them, the longsword over her shoulder.

"Almost time," someone from the hippie group called.

I turned to Toby and Heywood—and Pinscher, who had also somehow arrived at the meadow. "I need to do this alone," I said. With my tattoo starting to flare, I pulled the astrolabe from my backpack and nearly dropped it. Inching up the brass mechanism was a scarab.

While I was still reeling from what the beetle represented, someone grabbed at the astrolabe. Khufu, in a gilded robe, pulled at it, but I gripped harder and pulled too.

"You can't have it," I said, now afraid more for the astrolabe than for myself. Time was galloping past. The sun would spill through the Notch very soon.

"Leave her be." Toby matched Khufu in size but his advantage was passion. He jerked Khufu away from me, and I quickly knelt in the meadow, astrolabe hugged to my chest, and closed my eyes.

Someone was chanting down the seconds.

To myself—to the cosmos that surrounded me—I first made my apologies to Braden for failing him. Then, acknowledging Khufu's presence, I whispered softly, "Take me, Khepri, I bind myself to you. Release Parker Thomas, set him free."

A cheer arose as the Notch became illuminated, the sun hitting just the right angle to spill the light through the gap and out along a line in the meadow. The light cut me like a laser, flashing against my closed eyelids. I felt my body lift—or was I imagining that?

I was soaring above the Notch, my entire being filled with the power of the sun. The part of me that was in flight rotated before the solar orb, pieces of me glistening and shining as though I were covered in microscopic mirrors. The sun expanded, and its center began to seethe as a scarab crawled across it. The mirrors flashed, nearly blinding me. I tried to turn my head away or close my eyes, but it was impossible. Higher and higher I was drawn, as the sun and the scarab continued to wax until they filled my entire vision. No matter how I spun, the sun was everywhere and always.

How long did I drift in that state? Time had ended as a concept.

And then I was standing on a hilltop, the sun gone, the stars wild and thrashing overhead. In front of me, only a few yards away, a man reached out a thin arm through the bars of a wooden cage. His face was caked in dirt and sweat, his hair matted, and he wore nothing but a tattered pair of boxers. I almost gagged from the smell of rot and decay. He spoke words to me, but the thrashing of the stars drowned them out. The deep pools of his eyes pulled me toward him, but I was immobile again, frozen in place. Where had I seen that gaze before?

I fought against what bound me, but earned nothing in purchase but weariness.

Wait for the right moment. The thought glimmered dimly, a reminder from the past.

When? My mind screamed. *I've got to reach him.*

A star detached itself from the heavens and began an arced descent, spilling glistening stardust as it fell. A spangle of dust illuminated me for an instant, and my mind reacted. I thrust outward and my tethers burst, sending shards as sharp as knives.

"Watch out!" I shouted to the caged man, whose face I could almost remember.

But he was gone, and I lay on my back on the hilltop. The stars had faded into the sky's blackness, and I shivered in a cold wind that rustled the grasses around me. Overhead, the sun had returned despite the darkness. It lit up nothing. And this time, instead of expanding, it contorted, twisting and writhing as though in profound pain. Its prominences danced around the rim of the disk, moving faster and faster until one flung itself off with a howl into the blackness. Then another pulled off.

The man in the cage appeared, and his howls joined the cries of the sun.

The wind blew more strongly on the hilltop, and a terror seized me. My arms and legs—my entire body was on fire.

Stop, I cried out, but my voice wasn't working. *It hurts too much.*

Instead, a word in my head interrupted the sequence. It tried again and again to surface, and I finally let it and focused on it. *Formidable.*

My perspective shifted. I finally knew the answer to the puzzle. Sinking deep within myself, I gathered every inch of power, pulling it from each membrane, each cell, each atom, until I was filled and complete.

I am a conduit, I thought. I raised the astrolabe and sighted along it. The man in the cage turned his face toward me until his glittering eyes came into focus.

There was a sizzling burst of light, and I was back on the ground, in the meadow along the Brandywine Creek. So very cold on that humid June morning.

Hands helped me to a sitting position. It seemed I was surrounded by a crowd, but when I opened my eyes, the only face I focused on was my brother's, a real face, of flesh and blood, his outline firm and solid.

"QT," he said.

It had been a thousand years or perhaps a heartbeat. I tried once more to reach out to him, but the effort overwhelmed me, and I passed out.

Chapter 31

Some will say that what happened was a resurrection, but Braden and I both knew my brother was not dead. *Reunion* is the word I use—*to bring back together*. And in that meadow, under the rising sun, I wouldn't let go of my brother. Nothing else mattered. He laughed wanly at that, fine wrinkles etched around his eyes, a smile that also spoke of sadness and regret.

"Don't worry. I'm here to stay," he said, gently loosening my hand from his arm. His voice was rough, as though he hadn't said words aloud for an eternity. Wherever he had been left him thin and pale, a wiry beard streaked with gray, unkept brown curls falling below his ears. I sensed deep exhaustion flowing from him. One of Candi's Medieval friends wrapped a banner around him as a makeshift blanket.

"How long were you there?" I asked. It was a stupid question when I had so many more, but it was the first that came to mind.

He shook his head. "Too long."

Candi, Toby, and Heywood stayed a few steps away, unsure of what to do. Pinscher hung even farther back.

"My friends." I gestured at them for Parker, and they gathered around us. Then I remembered Khufu and tensed, glancing at the crowd that still mingled nearby.

Toby chuckled at my frown. "You should have seen her in action," he said. "Candi belted the sun guy with her sword, knocked him out cold."

"He's long gone," Heywood added. "The hippies threw him out when he came to."

I sagged with relief and hugged her. "You rock, girl."

Her eyes danced with glee. "I've wanted a reason to use it."

Turning to Parker, I rotated my forearm to show him the sun tattoo—*his* sun tattoo. "You've got to see this." But it had vanished completely, as though it had never been.

"It did its job superbly," Pinscher said in explanation. "You didn't need it anymore."

I looked from my brother to Pinscher. "But how did you know your sun sketch would…?" I let the question drift.

Parker shrugged. "I didn't."

"It was you," Pinscher said.

That I doubted. Whatever magical element Parker had unwittingly suffused into that slip of paper had made it possible for me to finally reach him. Wistfully, I looked at my arm. It felt naked without the sun, but my brother's actual presence made that unimportant.

Candi herded us all down the hill, along the narrow path, to our cars. She took my keys and slipped into the driver's seat. Toby took the passenger's side. "You two," she said to Parker and me. "Back seat. I'm driving." Buckled in, keys in the ignition, she turned around in her seat. "By the way," she said to Parker, "Happy birthday."

We ended up at Angelo's, an Italian restaurant that served Sunday brunch. Crowded around several tables, Candi's Arthurian friends dominated the room's conversation. They were there to celebrate — — what exactly, I wasn't sure.

To Heywood and Toby and Pinscher, I recounted what I remembered of what I called my trip to a mystical plane, as Parker sat silent, almost shell-shocked, beside me. His hands trembled when he used his fork and knife, but he dove into the food with an intensity that made me die on the inside. How long had he been trapped in that alternate world?

Pinscher, who sat to my left, murmured to me when I finished my tale. "I would be honored to take you on as an apprentice."

When I looked at him questioningly, he added, "Not for the tattoos, but for what can lie beyond them."

An appealing invitation. Perhaps I could really learn to marshal my emotional radar. "Let me get Parker patched up first."

He sopped up a bit of scrambled egg with his toast. "Of course."

The yellow of the eggs brought a fleeting image of Khufu grabbing the astrolabe. "Will the sun cult track him down?"

"They'll want you instead." He smiled at my reaction. "But you can handle them."

People kept peppering my brother with questions, and although he tried to offer answers, he became more and more edgy. "I can't talk about it yet," he said, frustration in his voice.

"Let's get out of here." I slipped enough money under my water glass to cover both of our meals and tugged on his arm. I waved at Candi, who tossed me my keys.

We sat in my car for a few moments while he leaned back with his eyes closed.

"That was harder than I thought it would be," he said.

"But you're here," I said. "You're alive."

"I'm fucked up." His eyes opened. "You should have left me. I'm not worth saving."

PTSD, I thought. *Depression*. He had a long road ahead, but I could help—had to help. I reached into the backseat for my backpack. "Let me show you something." I pulled out the sketchbook and laid it on his lap.

"Mine?" His eyes grew wide and he picked it up, holding it gingerly as if it were about to crumble. "You saved it?"

"Braden saved it. He said you left it for him when Dad threw you out."

"Yeah," he said, his voice going flat.

"Braden had it with him, one arm protecting it, when I found…" I couldn't finish the sentence. "He's going to be okay."

He turned the pages slowly.

"Damn," he said. "I was good, wasn't I?"

"You still are."

He sighed. "I haven't sketched or drawn for so long. I don't know if I still have it in me."

"I know it's too soon to think about it, but any idea what you'll do?"

He was still looking at the sketches, lightly touching the images of Braden, one by one. "I have no idea." He closed the book and let it lie on his lap. "I feel like I've been on an epic journey, like the sea voyagers in their sailing ships, finally finding their home port. I need to get my land legs back."

"I'm sorry you didn't get a chance to see Mom," I said.

"But I did," he said. The corners of his mouth turned up slightly. "You were there."

"You remember it?" He had been a shimmering image, standing at the foot of her bed.

"Of course. She was easing off the mortal coil." He said this without humor, just stating the facts. "It wasn't her fault, you know."

"She kept the letters you sent me, reading and rereading them. I finally found them just a few months ago."

His eyes showed surprise. "They never got to you?"

I shook my head. "Not a one. I thought you'd broken your promise."

"Never." He said this fiercely.

"Our family has been royally fucked up for a while," I said. "Good thing I'm a counselor."

It was much later that day, after Parker had fitfully dozed on and off for hours at my condo, that we made the trip to the hospital to see Braden. I had no idea how either one of them would react, and from the anxiety vibrating off Parker, I knew he had the same worry. It had been a decade since they'd seen each other. I considered my brother the extra lifeline Braden needed for the tough journey he faced. And Braden could provide the same for my brother.

The hallway at the hospital was quiet, visiting hours were nearing their end. The Hewitts were not in sight, so I pulled Parker inside Braden's room. Braden's eyes were closed, but he was vibrating a calmness, so unlike some our earlier encounters, when his energy level was off the charts. He was still hooked to the heart monitor, but his IV line was gone.

He must have sensed us, because he stirred and blinked open his eyes. When he found me, he smiled, but switched to a puzzled frown when he saw Parker.

"Yes," I said to Braden. "It's him. He's back."

The two men eyed each other silently for several moments.

"You've changed," Braden said at last. "You've grown up." He managed a chuckle. "So have I, I guess."

I left them alone to figure out their next steps.

Walking to the room from the hospital cafeteria with two cups of coffee, I savored the peace I finally felt. Sadness, of course, for my mother's passing. But hope now for a future for my brother—and with my brother. We had so much catching up to do.

Later that week, Parker sat beside me at our mother's memorial service. Toby claimed the spot to my right. Candy and Heywood sat in the pew behind us.

For the service, I'd written a short essay to read, second on the program after a family friend read one of my mother's favorite poems. My father sat across the aisle but in the same row of pews as Parker and me. He was with several neighbors and a few friends from his office.

The urn of my mother's ashes took center stage, surrounded by sprays of carnations and lilies. Photos of my mother were on display beside the urn. I had curated the photos at their house the same day I'd removed Parker's painting from the bedroom wall. My father nodded once at me as I left, the most he would acknowledge of my presence.

The pastor spoke of my mother's new home, and I closed my eyes. I preferred my mother be here, not in some stadium in the sky.

In the church hall afterward, people stood in small groups, talking quietly. The church volunteers had laid out a light lunch of small sandwiches and fresh fruit. I wasn't hungry, but Parker filled a plate, his body apparently still trying to close a deficit of calories.

My friends gathered around me. Across the hall, my father stood with the Hewitts and several neighbors, talking.

After a few moments, Roy Hewitt approached me. "I'm sorry about your mother," he said, giving me a hug. "She was a good person."

"Thanks. I'm so glad Braden will be all right."

"Yeah," he said, his eyes sliding away from mine. "Gail still seems to think you could have prevented what happened." He reflexively straightened his tie, rebuttoned his suit coat. "I'm sure you did all you could."

"He'd made up his mind," Parker said. "Nothing could change it."

"How do you know?" Mr. Hewitt said gruffly. "You weren't there."

"I know Braden, and I knew what he faced." Parker spoke with passion but kept his voice conversational.

"Yes, you did," Mr. Hewitt said, this time with a leer. "You certainly knew him."

"This is our mother's funeral," I hissed at him, taking Parker's arm and steering him away. Anger vibrated off my brother, growing stronger with every step. Over my shoulder, I said, "This is not the time for this discussion."

I nodded at Candi to let her know where I was going. Parker and I kept on walking, up the stairs, through the main hall, out the entrance doors, until we were standing in the parking lot.

"This is why I ran," he said, gesturing at the church, at the world. He leaned against my car.

"I understand." I put my arm around him again and led him around the building to the small graveyard at the rear. It was a close, overcast day. The air hung thick with humidity and a threat of rain, and I felt the dampness on the back of my neck. Parker loosened his tie and took off his suit coat. We walked past the graves and finally stopped at a massive stone cut with the form of birds and flowers. It was no one we knew, but a good spot to rest on and watch the sullen breeze lifting and moving the flowers that decorated a few of the graves.

"If only I had—" I started.

Immediately, he hushed me. "Sometimes we make the wrong decisions. Ones we can't take back." He paused. "Me, I was dabbler who got in over his head. You had the real stuff. I knew it when you were little—even before you knew, I'll bet."

I nodded. How can a child know that her normal isn't everyone else's?

Parker continued. "It wasn't until you and I were teens that I realized I could also dip into people's feelings. I think that's what drew Braden and me together."

We were just kids, Braden had said.

After a pause, Parker said softly, "We were in love."

"And now?" I blurted it out, but immediately worried that I had over-stepped, pushed too far.

Parker looked out at the graveyard. "It's too soon to know. I'll always love him, in some way."

"Did I tell you that Braden punched Dad?"

My brother returned from his reverie. "No way." When he saw confirmation in my face, he laughed out loud. "It's not funny, but it is. I'm assuming Dad deserved it—but a roundhouse? Braden?"

I filled him in on the details. The wind had picked up, threatening rain, but I didn't want to go inside.

"Where did you end up when you first left?"

"Here, there, wherever the road would take me."

"I saw your mural, in San Francisco."

He raised his eyebrows. "You did?"

"Online, when I was searching for you, after finding the letters and the weird sun. It was magnificent." I automatically touched my forearm where the sun had blazed. "And I went to Boston to see the scarab and then the pyramid in New York."

He nodded, absorbing that information.

"As I said, I was a dabbler," he said. "I wanted to think I was like you. And once I was on my own, I got it into my head that I had strength enough to take on the world. I barged into places where things can go south quickly. I got trapped by my own ego." His hands were shaking.

"But you're here now," I said. "That's what's important. You survived."

He stood away from the stone monument so he could face me squarely. "I survived because you have the power. It's *you* who saved me. Just as *you* saved Braden. Trust in yourself, QT."

Pinscher's exact words.

It was time to listen.

We waited at the church until my father got into his car and drove off. The predicted rain spattered the windshield as we followed him to his house and parked in front, along the curb. From there, I could see the third house down, where the Hewitts had lived all through my childhood, where I headed after school to hang out with Parker and Braden. I didn't know who lived there now. It didn't matter.

"Are you ready for this?" I wasn't sure I was ready, but it had to be done.

Parker sat in silence, looking out his window at the house. "I've dreamed about this for years. It never goes the same way twice."

In the steady drizzle, we got out of the car and walked to the front door. I could have delayed the confrontation, giving my father time to heal from my mother's passing. But his continued unwillingness to acknowledge my brother needed to end.

When I rang the doorbell, Gideon barked. Minutes ticked by, and I rang the bell again to more barking. Finally, I heard the lock unclick. My father stood in the doorway, staring at us.

When he made no move to open the storm door, I said, "Aren't you going to let us in?"

Still saying nothing, he pushed the glass door open, and I walked past him, with Parker just behind.

I surveyed the living room and chose the loveseat, wide enough for both my brother and me. My father shuffled in, his hands in his pants pockets. He was still dressed in his suit from the service, but he had removed his suitcoat and tie.

He looked at us, two dark-haired, lanky siblings with the same smile and the same brown eyes. His offspring, bound to him by our DNA.

"I suppose you're here for some kind of apology," he said, jingling the change in a pants pocket. I could see he was winding up for a lecture.

"No," I said. "It's too late for that."

He stopped jingling. "What then? Haven't you given me enough grief?"

"What about the grief you gave *me*?" Parker's voice was strangled in rage. "Ripping me away from the one person I loved so you could feel righteous and holy and all that crap."

I put my hand on Parker's arm, but he pulled away and stood. His hands were shaking again.

"And hiding the letters I sent to Quinn—I sent to *her*—so she never knew what happened to me."

"What letters?" my father said. The two of them were now face to face.

"And Quinn, treating her like she was some kind of satanic thing. She's the most brilliant person, with her ability—and you made her feel like she was nothing, over and over again."

"Parker," I said softly. "It doesn't matter anymore."

"I've waited years to say this to you, *Dad*." My brother had slipped into his old role as protector of his little sis. He would go toe to toe on my behalf. But I had learned much about myself over the last few months. I no longer needed his help.

I stood and took my place beside Parker. The emotional energy pouring off him almost pushed my father away.

"What I want to know," I said, piercing the rising anger in the room with an intentional calm, "do you have this power, too? Parker and I share this trait, so where did it come from? Mom said it wasn't from her."

My father seemed to crumple in on himself. He picked up a Bible from the end table nearest him and embraced it as though it were a protective shield. "It's evil. I cast it out from myself. Your grandmother … Her father … And on up the tree. I had to stop it."

He opened his Bible, found the page, and read. "For the just man falls seven times and rises again, but the wicked stumble to ruin." He raised his eyes to us. "I would not have wickedness in this house."

"We're your flesh and blood, your children," I said. "We aren't wicked, never were."

He grimaced as though tasting a bitter herb. "I saw those drawings, heard what the neighbors whispered. No, you were wicked." He pointed a finger at Parker, and turned it to me. "And you, with your secret eye that saw into the darkness and dwelt there."

I could sense the fear vibrating off him now. He was one against two — two baffling children who hadn't turned out the way he'd planned.

"You son of a bitch," my brother growled, his edginess erupting in anger.

I took a step closer to our father, and he raised the Bible again as a shield.

"You're right in your implication," I said. "We are different, maybe very different. And more important, different from you. But different doesn't mean evil. We just want to be loved for who we are."

I looked at Parker. The exhaustion he still battled was etched on his face, but he was calm again. He nodded, and we let ourselves out of the house, running through the rain, with our father standing alone in the living room.

Epilogue

Three weeks later, I was standing in Heywood's back yard in Morrisville. Another Sunday afternoon, under another cloudless sky, a typical July day in the mid-Atlantic region. The grill was fired up, ready for the burgers. Heywood had a red apron tied around his waist, poised to begin the cooking. First, though, he raised his bottle of ale.

"A toast," he called.

Candi adjusted the paper plates and napkins on the patio table, making sure they were perfectly aligned, then picked up her bottle. Parker was batting a volleyball over a make-shift net with Toby, and they both paused their toss. Pinscher and I stood under a maple tree that offered ample shade.

Absentmindedly I rubbed my arm where the sun used to be. I wished Braden was there, but his rehab would last at least another week or two. He'd made it this far, I knew he had a good chance to nail the rest.

"To Heywood and Thomas, shrinks for hire," Heywood said. He was wearing the Metallica shirt I'd presented to him when we'd signed the paperwork.

"Here, here," Pinscher responded.

"Thomas and Heywood," I countered.

"Alphabetical wins," Heywood said, holding his bottle aloft again for emphasis.

"Stand your ground, QT," Parker said, laughing. He was relaxed and rested. The nightmares that woke him screaming had eased.

We had an office, a few clients lined up, and a lot of work ahead. Somehow it seemed manageable.

After a picnic dinner complete with red, white, and blue streamers—it was Fourth of July weekend—we settled into the patio chairs to watch the fireflies and the occasional aerial display that arced high enough to clear the neighbors' roofs.

Heywood and Candi had their chairs touching, holding hands. *Finally a good match for her.* Toby sat to my left, Eddi on his lap, her eyes already closed in sleep. Where we would end up, I wasn't sure. I would take it one day at a time.

"Parker," Pinscher said, his feet propped up comfortably on a stool. The crab on his hand swiveled its eyes to me, as usual. "Your sister needs a new piece of ink since she lost the one you gave her."

I sputtered, "I didn't lose it. It disappeared."

"Can you draw her a new one?" Pinscher said.

"I'll pass," I said. I had no interest in another mystical emblem that burned and contorted, and invited odd creatures to my door.

"This one would be completely benign," Pinscher said. And added more quietly, "Your strength is now self-imbued, you know." And it dawned on me what he was up to.

"If he'll draw it, you'll ink it?" I said, leaning forward.

"Guaranteed."

"Parker?" I said, smiling. "Please?"

Parker closed his eyes briefly. *Give me the splendid silent sun,* he recited.

I took that as a yes.

Acknowledgments

NOTES

The line of poetry referenced by Parker Thomas is from Walt Whitman's poetry collection, Leaves of Grass. The individual poem is titled "Give Me the Splendid Silent Sun."

I owe a debt of inspiration to friend and colleague Brooke Wheeler, whose experience with the summer solstice "sun crack" in San Francisco gave me the idea for the fictional Brandywine Notch.

THANKS

This novel would not be possible without the support of a "village."

Thanks to fellow writers Kate Brandes and Janet Robertson, who read a very early version of this story and offered the encouragement to keep going.

Thanks to stellar editor Kathryn Craft, whose guidance, feedback, and suggestions helped this story grow and mature.

I'd like to acknowledge the expertise of Gene C W Taylor, M.S., MAC, who provided valuable details about addiction counseling; his wisdom and advice made this book so much better.

Thanks to fellow writer Peter J Barbour, a retired neurosurgeon, who offered feedback on my depiction of brain cancer and its treatment.

A big thanks to my publisher, Angel Ackerman, for taking on this project, and to proofer Allison Stein for her careful eye.

A special thanks for the support given by my Hive mates Diane Sismour, Jacqueline Day Pallone, and Catherine Jordan; by fellow writers Donna Galanti and Tori Bond, and by the members of the Bethlehem Writers Group.

Thanks to the national group Sisters in Crime for providing the many write-ins I attended to get this book finished.

And finally, thanks to Steve and Gabriel, for everything, always.

About the Author

Dianna Sinovic crafts absorbing stories of mystery, intrigue, paranormal, and fantasy. She also works as a book coach and editor, helping other authors realize their writing goals. When she's not at her keyboard, she can be found paddling a canoe on a winding creek, reading from her towering TBR stack, or baking another batch of cookies—preferably chocolate. She currently lives with her family in eastern Pennsylvania, with a pair of birding binoculars always close at hand. *Scream of the Silent Sun* is her debut novel.

Make a connection with Dianna on Substack!

https://diannasinovic.substack.com/

Leave a review on Amazon, Goodreads, or Google Books

Readers use reviews to find books.

Retailers' web sites use reviews as part of their algorithm.

Some advertisers require a certain number of reviews.

Share social media posts

Find Dianna virtually at

Instagram: @dsinovic94

Facebook: dsinovic

DO YOU WANT TO HELP PARISIAN PHOENIX OR ANY SMALL PUBLISHER OR INDEPENDENT AUTHOR?

- Buy books. Buy more books. Give books as gifts.
- Recommend authors to friends.
- Share Social Media Posts.
- Leave a review:

Amazon

Goodreads

Google Books

Learn how ➡

- Readers use reviews to find books.
- Retailers' web sites use reviews as part of their algorithm.
- Some advertisers require a certain number of reviews.
- Join and share newsletters.
- Attend events.
- Join Goodreads and follow authors, mark their books as read, shelve and rate them.
- Check on Patreon and Kickstarter for the creators you love
- Start a book club.

Subscribe to our Newsletter, "Bookish Babble", on

substack

https://parisianphoenixpublishing.substack.com/

www.ingramcontent.com/pod-product-compliance
Lightning Source LLC
Chambersburg PA
CBHW071930190726
48293CB00004B/1228